I0666800

Lock Down Publications and Ca$h Presents

FO'EVA ROLLIN' 4
SHADED TEARZ

Written By
Assa Raymond Baker

First Edition 2026

Printed in the United States of America

This is a work of fiction. Names, characters, places, and incidents either are products of the author's imagination or are used fictitiously. Any similarity to actual events or locales or persons, living or dead, is entirely coincidental.

Lock Down Publications
P.O. Box 944
Stockbridge, GA 30281
www.lockdownpublications.com

Like our page on Facebook: Lock Down Publications
www.facebook.com/lockdownpublications.ldp

Stay Connected with Us!

Text **LOCKDOWN** to 22828 to stay up-to-date with new releases, sneak peaks, contests and more…

Like our page on Facebook:
Lock Down Publications

Join Lock Down Publications/The New Era Reading Group

Visit our website:
www.lockdownpublications.com

Follow us on Instagram:
Lock Down Publications

Email Us: We want to hear from you!

Intro

It's day three of the fifteen-to-thirty days that I'd been awarded in the Restrictive Housing Unit, back on July 7th, 2022, for giving a young goofy a hard lesson in respect. Still can't believe the kid really thought he had a shot when he stepped to me like that. Bold, reckless, and stupid—but I'll give it to him: he had heart. And that alone earned him more credit than most.

Anyways, this morning—immediately after completing my personal workout routine of jumping jacks, pushups, and knee raises—the annoying sound of the officer tapping her key against the heavy steel door of my cell snapped me out of my mental zone.

"Shower?" she asked, barely able to peek through the window at me with her short self.

"Yes. Please." I locked eyes with the short, homely-looking snow bunny. It was clear that she'd been ogling my shirtless, sweaty, well-put-together, 225-pound, rich chocolate body long before she made a move to get my attention. Hey, I don't mind being her eye candy.

"Do you need soap?"

"No, I have my own." I quickly pulled on a shirt and gathered my things for the shower, then went over and put my hands through the tray opening in the door.

The officer carefully locked a pair of handcuffs around my wrists. She made sure they were not too tight, but secure enough, before unlocking and sliding open the door. Her soft hands clasped my left bicep firmly as she escorted me to the shower stall at the end of the range.

"Let me know if you need anything," she muttered after locking me in the stall and requesting me to place my hands out through the opening.

As she freed my hands, I had a brief fantasy of a few things she could give me in the shower. I flashed her a smile but said nothing. Once she moved on to go get the next man in line for a shower, I disrobed, tossed my dirty clothes out though the trap door, and turned on the shower. Setting the water temperature just the way I like it, I stepped beneath the normally soothing spray. Right now, I do not only need the shower to wash me clean, but to also help me to relax from a dream I'd had of the last night I spent with my dream girl.

It had been some years since I'd woke up in the middle of the night wishing that I was holding her instead of a damn pillow. That dream—me and her, together—left a hole so deep in my chest, it pushed me straight into my workout early, like I was trying to sweat the ache out. Shit hit me so hard, I damn near doubled my usual five hundred pushups just to keep from thinking. Now I'm standing under the hot spray, hard-ass water pounding on my bald head and shoulders, hoping it'll knock the memory loose and send it down the drain. When the officer called the two-minute warning, I rinsed off, killed the water, and stood there feeling the same way I did when I woke up from that fucked-up dream—empty.

"Aye, OG?" Duke called out to me as soon as I was back in my cell.

"Wudd up, lil bro?"

"You good over there? You looked like you had somethin' on your mind when you walked past just now, and I heard you up workin' out early as a bitch."

"I'm good over here. Listenin' to Bags' story just made me have a dream that brought up some old feelings, that's all."

"My bad, Assa!" Bags apologized, joinin' the conversation through the vent.

"OG, you know if you need to talk, I'm here. Sometimes an ear is all a nigga need to chase the blues away, and I got two good ones," Duke encouraged with a chuckle.

"Duke, yo' ass crazy," Bags exclaimed.

"Yeah, he is, but it's truth to what he said," I defended him as I took a seat beneath the vent so we could hear each other better. "Did I ever tell you about ol' gurl I was fuckin' with when I got locked up for this case?"

"Not really. You mentioned somethin' 'bout breakin' up with yo' girl when you got knocked, but that's it," Duke answered.

"Oh, well, she's the reason I was up early workin' out like that. I had a dream of her that got me over here missin' her. Man, y'all . . . if I could take back breakin' up with her because of this time I'm doin', I would. It seemed like the right thing to do at the time, but shit, now I'm wishin' I had all that time with her."

"Was she a bad bitch or what, OG? I'm guessin' she had to be, if you still thinkin' about her after all the years you got in now."

"She was all that. The crazy part about her is how we got together in the first place. It was some of that toxic love bullshit that Bags was talkin' about last night."

"Shit, you gotta tell me about that now. I might learn somethin' to help me hold on to my gurl."

"What was so toxic about y'all relationship?" Bags inquired.

"I ain't say shit about our relationship. We were good—it was the shit surroundin' both of us that was toxic. Hell, it's that bullshit that got me in the predicament I'm in now. Bro bro, y'all give me a minute. I'm finna make some tea right quick and I'll tell y'all."

They agreed. I went and made me a cup of Wyler's Light Lemon Iced Tea and folded up my blanket to sit on, then went back over to the vent.

"Let me see . . . I think it's best that I start from the day I got out from doin' my fed bit . . ."

Chapter 1

After serving almost every bit of the seven long years I was given in the feds, I got released at the beginning of August 2007. August's my birth month, so the gift of walkin' outta that hell house was the best gift I could think of receiving at the time.

But I wasn't really a free man.

I still had to do three years of supervised release after completing six months in a federal halfway house—'cause after bein' gone so long, I needed time to get reacquainted with my wife, D'Marie, and her old stompin' grounds on Milwaukee's deadly North Side neighborhoods.

I'd be a fool to think I could just step back into any situation I'd been away from that long. I know everything grows and changes—sometimes for the best, but sometimes not. Myself included.

Just as we had planned, my aunt and uncle were waiting for me where the crowded Greyhound bus pulled to a stop in Chicago. They picked me up there because the bus ride would've taken way longer to get me back to Milwaukee. Plus, I wanted some extra time to visit with my mother, who I hadn't seen the whole time I was away.

"Boy, get over here and give me a hug!" my Aunt Amy exclaimed as soon as she spotted me exiting the bus.

"Heeey, y'all!" I excitedly greeted, giving them both long, emotional hugs. "I've missed your hugs," I said before putting my big green, military-issued duffle bag in the trunk of my Uncle Ed's gleamin' champagne-colored, gold-trimmed Buick Lucerne.

The excitement of being on my way home, mixed with the anticipation of it all, had me ramblin' off non-stop questions until my uncle told me to shut the hell up and enjoy the ride.

"Nephew, yo' ass must've forgot that a nigga needs his driving music to stay focused on the road. Now sit yo' ass back, relax, and enjoy the ride," he said, then turned up the radio.

I did as I was told, layin' my head back on the soft leather seat. I let the soulful voices of the Isley Brothers help me ease my mind and enjoy the smoothest ride I'd had in years. As the Buick sailed down the interstate, the song "Contagious" brought up thoughts of my estranged wife. *"You're contagious, touch me baby, give me what you got . . . Sexy lady, drive me crazy, drive me wild."* I softly sang along, wondering how much bullshit, if any, D'marie had waiting for me. I thought of all the times that I had no idea how to reach her. All the times that I'd called her mother's phone, searching for my wife and baby girl, Ashley. Hell, the only reason that I was to see the estranged D'marie is because I'd sent her them divorce papers a few months back that made her get in touch with me and plead her case.

So, on that note, I really wanted to go to the halfway house so I could stack me some paper in case all that good shit she was talking was all talk, and I needed to start over on my own.

Our first stop when we made it back to the Mil was my Mom's crib. I needed to see her and hold her. I'd lost both my grandmother and stepfather not long before my release, so I knew she needed my hugs as much as I needed hers, since we were both pushing through the grief.

"I love you and I've missed you so much, but if you don't get your ass to that place, I'ma kick it there! I don't need yo' big head self getting in trouble before you even made it home all the way!" she scolded me immediately after getting' her hugs in.

"I'm not gonna get in trouble, Ma. I got plenty of time to get over there. I needed to see you before I turned myself in to the halfway house," I explained, then inquired about my younger brother and sisters' whereabouts.

"Sheka told me to tell you that her and the kids will be down to the halfway house to see you. They might already be there waiting on you. I don't know if Ville with her or not, but that's where he said he was heading when he left here," she answered, then ordered me to get on my way with the promise that she'd be there to visit me the next day.

With my mother's promise, I got back in the car with my aunt and uncle. We made my next and final detour to my wife's house. I call it her house, 'cause that's exactly what it was. She moved there while I was gone, so I've never been there before. I didn't have a say in her doing the move or any of the other choices that she made. So, no matter how you look at it, it's her crib, not mine or ours.

Not long after, Ed pulled the car to a stop in front of a nice-looking duplex home in a fairly decent area on the Northside. I got out, surveying the faces of the kids running around playing on the block, looking for any of ours. Not finding anyone out there, I jogged onto the porch and nervously rang the doorbell. A few moments later, I heard someone rushing down the stairs, then flipping the locks on the door.

"Guess who's back!" I sang looking in the face of my stepson. The big boy gave me an emotional bear hug. "Where's everybody?"

"Mama and nem went to the bus station to pick you up."

"Ah, damn, she's gonna be mad. Tell her my uncle came and picked me up in Chicago, so I'll have a little time to spend with everybody before I had to report to the halfway house."

"You can come in and wait 'til they get back."

"It ain't no telling how long she's going to wait down there, so I'ma just get on down to this place. Tell her she can come there as soon as she get back . . . if not, I'll call when I get settled in." I hugged him again and headed on into the halfway house, with almost an hour to spare.

The federal halfway house is locked smack dead in the middle of the hood, on 24th and Locus Ave. As many times I've been in this area in my life, I never knew this place was here. I shook my head at all of the illegal activities going on outside of the place. I kid you not, there's a dope house almost right next door to the place, with hypes and dope boys scattered up and down the block doing what they do to get what they wanted. They are all dumb as hell to be so close to the place doing anything illegal. That's them, it's not my life anymore. Their asses will learn the hard way, just like I had to.

Chapter 2

I got all settled into my new place for the next six months. It felt a little odd having the females wandering around me as freely as they were. We were allowed to fully interact with each other. We did everything with the females except shower and sleep. It was crazy.

The following day, D'marie was there to visit. I spotted her as she was checking in at the officer's desk. She was looking and smelling good when she hugged me, but when she didn't kiss me, I got a bit suspicious. She seemed to be on guard with me, which made me fall back and take a closer look at the way the visit was heading. It didn't help that she came to see me without the kids. I was disappointed because I really wanted to spend time with them, especially my daughter Ashley.

We found a table in the back of the visitin' room, which was also the chow hall. Even though there weren't many people there, I felt that we'd need as much privacy as the space would allow us. I was right to do this, 'cause D'marie skipped the small talk and came clean with me. She explained why she fell out of touch with me the way she had. She pointed the finger at me, blaming me for her absence. She said she was hurt 'cause a female I was fuckin' on before we got married was tellin' everyone who knows me that she has a baby by me and I was comin' home to them. This was news to me. I mean, I did know about the baby, but me comin' home to be with them was new. Hell, after I took the DNA test for the lil' girl, I never heard from them again.

"Bae, it's hard for me to believe anything with that bitch constantly throwin' that child in my face."

"I don't see what that has to do with me. I'm not tellin' her to do any of that shit. I don't have no reason to lie to you, and you know I'll never deny a child of mine . . . Like I explained to you when we started back talkin', Child Support said that they would only get in touch with me if I'm the father. I ain't got nothin' else from them, so I'm not." I took her hand in mine, looked her right in her eyes as I promised to get a copy of the DNA results as soon as I could.

"I'm lookin' like a fool to everybody for marryin' you the way I did, so you need to make this right. And you need to make that bitch stop her bullshit!"

"I don't know how to get in touch with the bitch, and I don't have a reason to. So unless you know where she at and 'bout to give me her address, how do you expect me to do that? I told you I don't talk to her."

"Once she find out that you're here, she might pop up on you so you can spend time with your second family."

"Stop it!"

"No, you stop her. Check her ass, don't try to check me. I'm your wife!" she retorted, releasing my hand and sitting up straight in her seat, glaring at me.

"D'marie, this ain't that. I'm not tryna check you. I'm just saying, stop with all that extra bullshit and trust me when I tell you that I'ma get the paperwork so we can put this behind us." We sat in silence for a few moments. Studying her eyes, I could see that she was trying to find the courage to say her next words.

"What else on your mind?" I inquired, ready for her to say that she wanted out of the marriage. I was good with that, 'cause it wasn't like she was an active wife anyway.

"Bae, you said that you understood that I was messing with someone else while you were in the other place, but now you're out and…"

"But nothing!" I interrupted. "I told you when I got my time exactly what I expected of you. The issue is you let that nigga come between us."

"No, your bitch came between us!" She raised her voice, but not high enough to draw much attention to us.

"This ain't my first bid. I know better than to put my time on you." I took her hand back in mine, pulling her closer before I spoke. "I'm not tryna fight with you, Dee. You're my wife and I'm tryna move forward from here. I only wanna make you happy and work toward spending the rest of our life together. That can only happen if we stop looking behind us."

"I hear you talking, but you gotta show me that I'm still what you want. That we're still what you want. I don't need you coming back in my kids' lives if you're not sure you wanna be with us. That's not fair to them." She was crying now. I mean laying it on real thick.

From the way the visit was going, I could tell that I wasn't gonna be getting no sexual healing from her no time soon. I told her we should use my time in the halfway house to get to know each other all over again. When she agreed, that pretty much ended the visit. I was mentally exhausted. She promised to bring the kids to see me the next time she came, and with that, I walked her to the door.

Chapter 3

By me not being able to move around the way I needed to in order to produce the DNA paperwork the wife need for us to put this whole baby thing behind us, we was pretty much on shaky ground. Hell, half the time I couldn't get her on the phone. She either didn't answer or was too busy to talk. I ain't gon' lie, I was past frustrated with her holdin' that baby bullshit over my head. I couldn't tell if the stuff she was doin' was her dumbass way of testin' me or somethin'. I swear, walkin' away from it all was lookin' better and better by the day.

I believe it was on a Wednesday afternoon when the job coordinator came through in desperate need of someone who wasn't afraid to get their hands dirty. Even though I'd been warned by others about the job, I took my chances. Because he really needed a worker, the halfway house viewed the wait time for me to be able to go out and get a job.

"How much do this dirty, funky job pay?" I didn't really care as long as I was able to get passes from the halfway house to move around almost every day. The job coordinator tole me the pay started off at $8.50 an hour, with a nice raise if I stayed. There wasn't any more to think about for me. I signed all of the paperwork he needed me to sign. Hell— after working my ass off for .25 cents per hour in prison, $8.50 felt like I hit the lottery.

The added benefits that came with having a job was: getting my own room, and more important was being able to get passes to go home for overnight stays. Needless to say, a few days after I started the job, I started sneaking over to my wife's house every morning before I went in to work. All we did was talk, which was a pure tease—seeing her half-dressed and still not giving me the goods. Knowing how she likes to fuck, I started guessing that she still messing with the dude she was with while I was away. With that thought, I started messing around with this woman I met on a date line. Her name was Angel, which fit her perfectly, because she was a blessing to me after being teased by D'marie for all that time, and on top of the almost seven-year sex drought I'd went through in prison.

Angel had a car, so our first meeting was her picking me up after I went to get my State ID. I knew she really liked me from the phone sex we had the night of our first face-to-face. I let her know I wasn't with all that teasin', and she assured me there were no games with her. The next mornin', she picked me up from the gas station behind the bus stop on 35th Street. I spotted her black Chrysler sittin' in the gas station lot way before she noticed me walking up and tapping on her window.

As far as her looks go, she wasn't a dime, but she was far from ugly. She had a sexy, exotic look to her that told me she'd be fun. Angel was about five foot five, with a medium, curvy build. Her long, honey blonde locks blended perfectly with her golden skin complexion. She was in her late forties, which made her over ten years older than me, but she didn't look it at all.

"If I ask you somethin', would you be honest with me?" she asked as she pulled away from the gas station, heading to her house.

"I haven't lied to you yet, so why start now?" I replied, looking at her from the passenger seat.

"Am I what you like or is this gonna be a polite one-time booty call?"

"Well, the booty call part is on you. You picked me up, not the other way around. And yeah, you're still what I like.

My attention to you is real. I don't care how long I've been away, I ain't just gonna go for anything. You're the one who wants to experience some of this fresh-out-the-pen beef, and I plan on bringing your fantasy to life by giving you every hard inch of it." I shot her a mischievous smile that made her blush.

Angel pulled the car to a stop in front of a big two-family home that she owns, then boldly leaned over and kissed me. I kissed her back. At this time, I'd been out for over a month and my wife wasn't tryna give it up. When the kiss ended, I glanced at the clock on the dash and saw I had almost two hours before I had to be at work. She only lives about ten minutes on foot from my job, so I had plans to make the time count. Hey, you know how it goes, what one woman won't do, another one would—and more.

The interior of the home was nice. Angel had very good taste and an eye for style. The way she dressed and the way her home was decorated would make you think she worked as a stylist instead of a substitute grade school teacher. Then again, during our many late-night phone conversations, she did mention that she was working on a clothing line, so it fits her. I followed her lead, taking off my shoes at the door so we wouldn't track the dirty rainwater on her nicely polished hardwood floors.

Angel took my hand and towed me right inside her bedroom. I asked her for the dance she promised me the night before and made myself nice and comfortable on her super-soft queen-sized bed.

"I didn't promise you a striptease. I said a dance. It's a difference."

"Okay, but your words left it all to my interpretation, and right now I wanna see your sexy self dance, shuu and strip for me."

She glared at me for a moment, then slowly sashayed her way over to the stereo. She put on some soft, soulful music I never heard before and began dancing for me. She did this slow hip roll with each movement suggesting more to come. As she began removing her clothing slowly, it was frustratingly sexy. Angel's body was much better than I expected it to be outta her clothes. I couldn't stop watching her alluring hips and thighs. I quickly stripped down to my boxer briefs and laid back on the headboard to better enjoy the show she was putting on, as she slowly and provocatively approached me.

"Is that for me?" she pointed at my erection.

"Only if you want it." I removed my boxers so she could get a better view of what awaits her.

"Ummmm, can I show you how much I want it?"

Before I could reply, she put her soft, warm, wet mouth around my tip. I knew right then that she knew just what she wanted and what to do with it. I'm tellin' you, that woman licked, sucked, and slurped her place in my memories forever. Angel's lips and tongue made me erupt almost instantly, but she stopped sucking and started stroking it with fast, erotic gestures. When she combined that with her wet mouth, all of what I had been longin' to release for almost seven years burst out of me, spilling right out on her lips and chin. No, she didn't swallow, but she didn't stop suckin' until I was nice and hard again.

Our eyes met, and she gave me this mischievous smile. I pulled her all the way onto the bed with me. Immediately, I ran my hands across her hairless mound, parting her luscious lips. I ran my finger over the hood of her clit and down through the slick folds. When I pressed two fingers inside her, she started gaspin' and hummin' as her warm cum coated my hand. I tossed her legs over my shoulders and rammed my length in her until I hit home.

"Uh, oh fuck!" she cried out. "Get this pussy, Assa, fuck me hard. I'm yours. Shit, babee, I'm yoursss!"

Chapter 4

Driving in hindsight, if I'd known then what I know now about D'marie, I would've focused more on me and lived that bachelor's life. But moving on, I only told you about Angel so you'd know that I was about ready to wash my hands off my estranged wife. I knew she was on some bullshit for real when she never said a word about me not dropping by in the mornings before work. Yeah, I was spending a lot of time in Angel— I meant with Angel. Okay, it was both. If it wasn't for the promise I made to give things with my wife a real chance and the promise I made to the children, I would've been with Angel. But blind loyalty kept me stuck here.

Angel was so cool and level-minded that when I was finally granted my overnight pass from the halfway house, passes that I had to take at D'marie's crib because it was listed as my home address, Angel didn't even trip on me a little. When I called her and explained the rules of the pass, all Angel asked was if I'd be in the bed holdin' her on Monday morning. She didn't blow up on me nor show one ounce of jealousy. All I heard in her voice was a little disappointment, which I fully understood.

Do I really need to go into every detail of what happened at my estranged wife's house when I took that first overnight pass? How about I just skip to this. Sometime between midnight and two in the morning, D'marie and I started working on patchin' things up between us. After making her remember my name, she confessed about her little financial problems.

"I'm so ashamed and embarrassed to be where I'm at in my life right now, when you had everything set up for us before you left us," she said, cryin' real tears.

Being the man that I am, I did what I had to do to get the house caught up and current on the bills. And I proudly did it without doing anything that would've gotten me a new case. I put in a bunch of overtime hours at work and manipulated a few numbers on my checks so the halfway house wouldn't trip on me for not giving them all of my money, and got it done.

Because of the moves I'd made something deep inside me told me to keep Angel around, just in case things caught up with me and the wife broke bad on me. I'm a real thug with good hustler's intuition. I believe if someone does some foul shit in the past, it'll be dumb to put all my trust in them again. Not saying that my full trust is given to anyone in the first place. Trust is to be earned and it takes work to be kept.

Now, skippin' ahead some. As soon as I completed my halfway house time and was released home to D'marie and the kids for good, I lost my job. If I didn't know better, I would've thought it was all by design. I didn't trip on it, I just got on my grind. My legal grind to keep cash flowin' in. Directly after losin' my job, D'marie somehow got into it with my daughter Nina's mother. I don't even know how they got each other's numbers.

"Reign, what do that bitch mean that I'ma always be second to her? Be honest, nigga, is you still fuckin' her?" D'marie snapped.

After a long, stressful day of job searchin', I'd returned to the house to some more stressful bullshit.

"Dee, you trippin' fo' real," I calmly said, walkin' past her and into the kitchen, lookin' for somethin' to snack on until she made dinner.

"Answer the fuckin' question, nigga, are you still fuckin' her?" she demanded, followin' close behind me like a crazy person.

"I'm not finna go back and forth with you. If I had somethin' to hide, she wouldn't be callin' the house." To be real with you, I was throwed off by the confrontation. I'd never witnessed her act like this with me. My first pure thought was that she was pickin' with me to take the heat off of somethin' she's doin' or about to do. "You're doin' all of this over my daughter wantin' me to bring her sister over for a sleepover. How do you get me fuckin' her mother from that? Do you understand how stupid that sounds?"

"Mothafucka, don't call me fuckin' stupid!" She suddenly rushed me with her hand raised. I quickly backpedaled out of her reach. "So you really gonna stand in my face takin' up for that bitch? You're in my house talkin' shit to me and takin' her side over mine?"

"I ain't takin' nobody's side, because it ain't no side to take. I'm just sayin' that my daughter…"

Bam! She cold-slapped the next words right outta my mouth. After doin' so many years locked in a hostile environment, my instant thought was to strike back, but I quickly remembered she was my wife. I shook it off and put some more distance between us. When I did that, and she saw that I wasn't gonna hit her back, she got more animated and bold. She went to callin' me outta my name, swingin' wildly at me. I took a few more hits before I'd had enough and put a stop to it. Timed her next swing and easily sidestepped it, while at the same time grabbin' her forearm. I spun her to me, kickin' her feet from under her and firmly sittin' her on the floor…

"Don't fuckin' get up!" I barked angrily, glaring at her, sitting in shock at my feet. She's lucky I don't take after Ike Turner. "You know what, fuck this!" I turned and quickly left the house.

I was so mad that I walked over a mile to my mother's house. About halfway there, I calmed down some and went to thinking about how I could get some fast cash until I locked down me another job. As much as I was trying to do everything to avoid getting back in the game, it seemed like I was being pushed to the point of having no other choice but to pick back up a sack. I mean, I'm a whole boss ass nigga out there walking and on the bus and shit. I knew all I needed to do was say the word, and AR, the boss, was back on top.

When I reached my mother's, I saw that her car wasn't in the driveway, so I sat on the porch. I was just chillin', contemplating my next move while surveying the neighborhood. That's the first time I saw Mica. There was something about her that I couldn't take my eyes off. I found myself smiling, watching her trying to unload her grocery bags from her car while tryin' to coach a reluctant child to go in the house.

The woman looked like she could use a helpin' hand, so I got up to go lend her one. I wasn't sure if she noticed me strolling toward her because her focus was on gettin' her son to obey her. He was clearly purposely being a pain. Mica had finally had enough because she put her bags down on the concrete steps leadin' up to her house and firmly grabbed her son's arm while silently cursing her baby daddy for spoiling him.

"Listen, JoJo!" she snapped through gritted teeth. "I've had enough of your mess! Get up!" He didn't move. "If you don't get up and get yo' lil ass in the house now, I'm finna leave you out here so that big dog right there can get you," she threatened, pointin' at a big ugly, battle-scarred pitbull that was half-dragging its master down the block.

I kinda was on the little boy's side. I could understand why he was throwin' a full-blown temper tantrum. It was a beautiful day out, not too cool, not too hot, just too nice to be cooped up inside a house. I was almost to them when a slim, grimy, thugged-out dude appeared from Mica's gangway. Whoever he was, she didn't look happy to see him. He said somethin' to the guy walkin' the dog, then him and Mica instantly got into an argument.

The way he grabbed her told me that he was her dude. I slowed my approach because she now had a more pressing person to focus her energy on, especially since the dude was now creatin' more of a spectacle than her child had been. Another young boy, a little older than the one already outside, appeared on the porch with a miniature basketball that, after one dribble, went bouncin' and rollin' down the steps and right out into the street. Without the slightest bit of hesitation, JoJo broke free of his distracted mother's grip and went runnin' in pursuit of the ball.

I saw this at the same time I noticed a flashy, multi-colored SUV speedin' toward the child. I broke into an all-out sprint, reaching the boy just as the SUV's driver braked hard, causin' its twenty-six-inch tires to scream to a sliding stop. But not before it knocked me on my ass.

Mica and her dude clung to one another in astonishment. They were both unable to move. The terrified mother didn't breathe again until she saw her son walk from around her car, holding his scraped, bloody arm. He was crying . . . from where I'd tossed him out of the way and gotten myself hit instead. She ran to her son, scooping him up into her arms, thanking God that he was safe. When she turned to get a glimpse of me, the person who saved her child's life, she wanted to come over to see if I was okay and to thank me, but her guy wasn't havin' that. He pretty much dragged them in the house.

I was good for the most part. I just had the wind knocked outta me. I was good for real. The driver got out, checking on me and apologizing. When he saw that I was okay, he reached in his pocket and shoved a wad of cash in my hand, apologizing some more before we went our separate ways.

My mother was suddenly there cracking jokes about how many times she'd told me not to play in the streets. Ha-ha-

ha, she's a funny lady. I just wanted to lay down, so I had my mother drop me back off at the crazy lady's crib, hopin' that she'd gotten over what she was goin' through earlier. D'marie gave me the royal treatment when I walked through the door because my mother had called her and told her what happened. I know she was thankful that I was in one piece, but more thankful that I had come back after the way she acted earlier. As I was laid back on the bed, cummmin' down her throat, I forgave but didn't forget.

Chapter 5

Thunderous sounds of gunfire from the *Black Opps* wargame battle echoed through the house, adding to the internal flame that's been steadily darkening Mica's heart for the good-for-nothing manchild in the living room of her home.

After feeding and putting her son to bed, Mica stood at the kitchen sink doing dishes and thinking about how close she had come to almost losing one of her babies. For the hundredth time since the incident with her son and the SUV earlier that day, she thanked the Lord for sending her me, the unknown man who had risked his life to save her son's. Once finished with the dishes, she tied her mass of fine braids back with a hair tie as she walked toward the front room. Inhaling deeply, she thought about going back in the kitchen and arming herself with a knife but let the thought go with her exhale.

Mica stood glaring at the man who claimed to love her and care so much about her and the kids, but didn't move an inch to save her baby from the speeding truck. Knowing what she had to do, a sudden intense feeling of fear involuntarily caused her to forget to take her next breath. At 29 years old, Mica was so over being in this lonely, loveless, controlling relationship. After what almost happened because of his insecurities, she totally despised the punk sitting in front of her playing her kid's Xbox.

"You think I'm a silly bitch, huh!" she shouted, stepping closer to the source of her unhappiness. When he didn't respond, she moved closer and got louder. "Fuckin' look at me when I'm talking to you! I . . . I'm tired of this shit!" she stammered. "I'm done!"

"Bitch, what the fuck is you talking about?" he responded without pausing his game.

"I'm talking about you! I'm done with yo' fool ass and I want you to get your shit and leave!" she stated firmly. Before she could form her next words, the punk had sprung from his seat on her sofa and backhanded her so hard that she saw stars.

"You think you runnin' something up in here, huh? You think you can talk to me any kinda way!" he yelled, snatching her by her hair, then commenced to hitting her again and again.

*   *   *

That next morning, I woke up to an empty bed. Being a hunnid with you, I was glad D'marie had found something else to do, 'cause I was sore from getting hit by that truck. On top of that, I was still groggy from the make-up sex she insisted on having that lasted well into the late hours. I swear, it seemed like as soon as I closed my eyes good, again she pops up.

"Bae . . . Bae . . . Moe's here for you."

"Why, why, why!" I grumbled in frustration. "Tell him I'm still sleep," I replied over my shoulder, not knowing that she had brought him in the room with her to get me up.

"Yo' ass ain't sleep no mo', nigga, get up!" Moe ordered, slapping my feet to make me get a move on it. "C'mon, get up, bro bro, I need you to come ride with me down to the city, so I can link up with my plug," he explained when D'marie left us alone to finish with breakfast. "All he say he got left is my order and he need my bread so he can go do his thang."

"Yeah, I hear you. I hear you, but you said all that without saying why you need me to go down there with you. I told you already that I ain't tryna fuck with the game no mo'."

"Whateva, nigga. You ain't got shit to do now that you ain't workin', and I know you need the cash. So get the fuck up and c'mon. I don't trust nobody like I trust you to have my back. Now get yo' ass up an' get it together. I'ma be out in the car smokin'."

I watched him exit the bedroom. I took a fast shower, then got dressed in a simple black Dickies pants and shirt outfit. The only thing that wasn't Dickies was my shoes. I put on a pair of black Nike Air Max. The shoes were a gift from my sister as a thank you for fixing her car.

"Dee, I gotta make a run down to Chicago with Moe right quick to help him with somethin'." I said it like this, knowing since she knew that's where he's from, she wouldn't think too much of it. I didn't feel like hearing her mouth about us being broke. "I don't know how long it's finna take us, but I'll call when I get there and when I'm on my way back. I left money on the nightstand for you to do whateva with."

"Okay, bae. Be careful! Wait, here, eat." She shoved a paper plate with a nice home-cooked breakfast sandwich on it.

Outside, Moe was waiting for me in the passenger seat of his girl's forest-green Ford Taurus, which told me that I was driving.

"What you limpin' fo'? What happened?" he questioned when I dropped into the driver's seat.

"I got hit by a car yesterday over by Mama's house."

"You got hit by a car? What the fuck!" he exclaimed as we pulled away from the house.

"I'm good. I didn't get hit like that, it just knocked me on my ass. But I saved this lil' boy who'd ran in the street chasing a ball from gettin' ho'd, so yeah."

"Bro, you're a better man than me. Fuckin' with me, being there at that time, the lil' hard-headed muthafucka would've been pancaked. Straight up!" he joked, chuckling hard. "I know his mama gave you some thank-you head, or an IOU on the pussy or somethin' for damn near getting killed for her kid?"

"Maan, I didn't even get a good lookin' out from her or her nigga, now that you mention it. Then it was because of her guy that the lil' boy got away from her and ran out in the street in the first place. The nigga came out on some weak-ass shit with ol' girl that had distracted her an' shit."

"How did you know all of that? Did you know her? Let me find out you got one on the side."

"Naw, I was just close by, and unlike you, I pay attention to shit."

"Yeah, right!" he laughed. "Say, bro, on some real shit, what you finna do until you land another gig?" he inquired, stabbing out the rest of the blunt that had been smoking.

"Man, I don't know. I'm kinda thinkin' about going to see if Uncle Ed got something for me to do at the yard."

"That's wassup, go get on yo' Junkyard Dog, Sanford and Son shit," he teased. "You know unc cheap-ass ain't gonna pay you but a few pennies, so stop it. Bro, you know if you need somethin', anything, I got you. I'ma hit yo' hand for makin' this run with me too."

"That's wassup. I can use the money. Keepin' it a hunnid with you, this square life ain't easy as a muthafucka may think. I can't just cash out on some random shit whenever I want to. I always gotta be thinking about what's needed most in the household." I admitted as I turned onto the freeway onramp heading toward Chicago.

"You get it, bro bro. You just ain't cut for workin' fo' another muthafucka and livin' check to check. You need to have yo' own shit. It's hard to go from having' it your way, to livin' from check to small-ass fuckin' check. I told my plug 'bout you and he really wants to meet you, if you tryna fuck around?"

"So that's why you want me down there with you, huh?" I shook my head. "It's tempting as hell, but I got three years of fed paper that I'm walkin' down. You're lucky I'm takin' this trip with you."

"Yeah, I know, but before you say no, just think about what you can do with a quick flip or two," he suggested, then unpaused the song, *Spit Your Game*, by Notorious B.I.G.

We rode, grooving to the music. The whole time, I really thought about what he said and the way things was going for me. It'll only take a few good flips for me to get enough cash to start selling cars. Which I thought would be a nice little side hustle while I'm working whatever job I find. I really thought hard on it as I navigated through traffic. Just before we made it to the first toll booth, I had my mind made up.

"Did you tell yo' guy what I used to do?" I inquired after turning down the radio.

"Yeap. That's why he wants to fuck with you. His people be flooding him and he needs muthafuckas on his line that can really move weight fast."

"So this is the real reason you want me to come with you, you sonuvabitch!" He just smiled. "Okay, tell yo' guy I'll have a conversation with him since I'm already down here, but I'm still undecided on if I'm ready to jump in the game fo'real."

Chapter 6

Tired of being a punching bag and living in fear of her boyfriend's sporadic mood swings, Mica stared at her busted up reflection in the bathroom mirror. Her face was a mess, eyes red from cryin', cheeks all swollen from the last round. But in that moment, something inside her clicked. She wasn't gonna take no more of this shit. She wiped the last of her tears away, steeled herself, and swore to herself she'd never let him put his hands on her again.

Four hours later, she lied and told him she had a doctor's appointment for one of her sons, knowing damn well he wouldn't insist on tagging along. He was too scared the doc might call the cops and have his ass locked up once he saw Mica's bruised face. So, after dropping her son off at his grandma's, she picked up her sister for backup. But the truth was, she wasn't at no damn doctor's office. She was headed straight to the Milwaukee County Safety Building.

Mica didn't know what else to do, so she went there to obtain an order of protection. An hour or so later, she walked out armed with a restraining order and a half-ass promise that the police would be out to her home as soon as they could to order him to stay the fuck away from her and her children. But even with that piece of paper in her hand, Mica felt no safer than she did before.

"That shit was a big waste of time. Them bitches ain't about to do shit until they're good and ready!" Mica's sister vented once they were getting in the car.

"Hopefully the restraining order will scare him."

"Or make him beat yo' ass again for going to get it," Latici snapped. "That punk-ass paper order ain't finna scare nobody!"

"It might give me some time to figure something else out. It may give me time to move into another house or something!" Mica voiced her confusion as she drove home.

"Sis, you don't have to run from him." Latici got quiet for a moment, then all of a sudden said, "Mica, we should jump his punk ass!"

"Yeah, we should." Mica agreed, giving her sister's suggestion some serious thought. "We can catch him by surprise and bam! Knock his ass the fuck out with somethin'," she added, briefly daydreaming about punching him in the head and face repeatedly the way he had done her.

What started off as just a venting session had turned into them really scheming on the best way to get Mica's revenge without seriously getting themselves hurt in the process.

*   *   *

After two rainy hours . . . after we made the rendezvous with Moe's plug and took care of business, we were back on the road, leaving the South Side of Chicago now loaded with two and a half bricks of soft white work. I ain't gone lie, I had a new beat to my heart because the half kilo was all mine, free and clear. It was a gift from the plug, welcoming me to the team. Now, I hope you know I am far from foolish. You can't make me believe that was a "gift"—that's all it was. Truth be told, it was a hook test to see how long it would take me to get it gone and to see how I conducted business when I came back to see him.

The drizzling rain had stopped as soon as I made that right turn onto I-94, heading back up to the Mil. While sitting in stop-and-go, bumper-to-bumper traffic, I got to internally putting together a plan to get the work gone as fast as I could while at the same time maximizing my profit. The only thing

I knew for sure was I was keeping it a secret from D'marie. I had to concentrate on stacking me some rainy-day funds, just in case. Anything could happen in the game, and I needed to have something to fall back on when it did.

Moe's peer pressure came at the perfect time for me to give in and step back into the game. Things were drying up in the hood because of the feds, and because of that drought, I was able to almost double up that half a kilo. I made a quick fifteen geez to rush back to the plug with, on top of opening up a trap house that I immediately had dumping dime bags of crack like it was the '90s again. The streets missed me, because not only did I run through what I had, but I also got off most of bro's work too. The plug was highly impressed with the double trip that day, so much so that he hit us with five bricks and instructed us to take our time. I did the opposite with my two of the five. I whipped it up to four, sold three whole for a nice profit, then ran back down to the Chi alone to do business with some Lords I know over on the West Side. They showed me that brotherly love, and I returned to the crib with five bricks of my own.

* * *

While I was in the kitchen of my trap house making sure my whip game was still proper. I had to be extra careful with it because I had a P. O. who was by the book and too many people depending on me for me to slip up in any kind of way.

But anyway, while I was on that, Mica's dude had come to her crib, slightly staggering drunk and ready to issue out his verbal assault for the evening. When BG entered the house and laid eyes on Mica's sexy body, which was being illuminated by the light from the TV in the otherwise dark house, his thoughts changed from *fight* to *fuck*. However, Mica had other plans for him in mind.

She pretended to be asleep on the sofa. She was half-dressed in only a sports bra and sexy little boy shorts that she knew he liked to see her wearing. She peeked, watching him through tightly squinted eyes as he came closer. Mica felt a little nervous, but she was ready to do what she had to do to stop the torture and pain that she'd endured from BG for far too long.

"Aye! Let's go get in the bed . . . Mica! Mica, I said get up and let's go to bed!" he demanded, running his hand up her bare, thick chocolate thigh, then smacked her hard on her butt.

At the sound of the smack, Latici rushed from the closet behind him, where she'd hidden when they heard him working on the locks to get in the house. Without a word, she whacked him across the shoulder and again across his head with a table leg that had been broken off an end table the last time he had beaten her sister.

BG howled and clutched his head in pain. At that same time, Mica sprang up from the sofa, wildly swinging a cast-iron skillet at him.

"Bitch!" she shouted, slapping him in the face with the heavy skillet. "I hate you!" she repeated over and over with each swing.

Unable to defend himself against their perfectly planned attack, BG dropped to the floor and covered his bleeding head with his arms the best he could while crying and pleading for them to stop, the same way he had made Mica do many times before. By the time the police were called to the house, he was semi-conscious and very bloody.

"I see here you have an order of protection against him," an officer confirmed. "Tell me what happened here tonight."

"My sister and I were just sitting here talking when he came in upset."

"Excuse me, how did he get inside? Did someone let him in or . . . ?"

"He never gave me my key back when I told him to leave after the last time he jumped on me."

"Okay, so what happened once he got inside?" the officer inquired while scribbling Mica's statement in his notebook.

"I could see that he had been drinking. I told him to leave, and that's when he pushed me by my throat and slammed me into the wall." Mica pointed to the damage to a spot in the wall that had been damaged in a previous fight with BG. "He was about to hit me again when my sister found something and hit him with it to get him off of me. He let me go and went after her, so I ran and grabbed the first thing I could find," she lied, feeding the police officer the story just the way they had rehearsed it after they had taken the law into their own hands to stop the threat.

"Okay . . . I have what I need. Someone from the D.A.'s office will be in touch with you soon. Until then, he will be held in custody. If you don't have anything else to add, we're going to go. Enjoy the rest of your night."

"I will. Thank you! Mica replied, breathing a sigh of relief as she watched the police haul her trouble away.

Chapter 7

By the end of the month, my bank accounts were up. I'd bought myself a car and a truck, put my wardrobe back together, and made plans to open a used car lot. Yeah, I was feeling like my old self again. But that's not how I needed to feel, 'cause my old self is the version of me that got me thrown in federal prison. I quickly checked myself and focused on laying down the groundwork for my car lot. I still had to keep my P.O. happy so he'd stay off me. So, I started working as a bouncer for a few of my guy's nightclubs and private parties.

I was foolish to believe I could keep moving like I was without D'marie finding out. So, to keep down her bitchin', I called myself trying to do something nice for her on Valentine's Day. Since she didn't know I was back hustling good, my splurging had way more meaning to her than it would have if she did know. But even still, right after our special romantic weekend, I returned home one night to get ready for work at the club and found D'marie on some cold bullshit with me.

"Do you expect me to fuckin' believe that you get up and leave this house every gotdamn morning with your guys and come back at night with nothin'? Okay, I'll play Boo Boo da fool with you on that shit! Nigga, I know you. I know you're not just leavin' this house to help your guys for handouts while they line their pockets. You comin' in here giving me chump change. It ain't that much brotherly love in the world when you're broke!"

"What the fuck you on right now? Gurl, I don't gotta report to you my every move."

"I got yo' girl, nigga!"

"Whatever. I leave this house running from place to place looking for a job every damn day. On top of doing lil' odd-ass jobs to keep a lil' change in my pocket, then I share with you," I stood up from putting on my shoes and closed the space between us. "I told you this before, and I mean it. How bro-nem livin' ain't how I'm tryna live anymore. I'm on somethin' bigger and better. Let's not forget I just did seven long-ass years in a ruthless federal prison. If I don't move wise, I'm going straight back. I don't got no mo' time to give up. But fuck that. If me wanting to live better for my family is bum shit, then you're the one whose priorities are fucked up, not me."

"I don't know what happened to you in prison, but I didn't marry a scary-ass nigga. You need to get your shit together fast! I'm not gonna be takin' care of no grown-ass man when I got my kids to slave for!"

"What do that mean?"

"It means, nigga, you need to find yo' some place to go," she confirmed, then walked away from me.

"So, what, you puttin' me out? Dee, you act like I ain't been giving you money for shit around here. You seriously puttin' me out?"

"Yeah. Maybe you'll get your shit together."

"Wow, a'ight . . . That's fucked up. Fuck this, you can trust and believe I ain't gonna be down foreva. You say you know me, then you should know better."

I wanted so much to slap her ass with the ten geez I had in my glove compartment and be like... "Who you callin' broke, bitch!" But nah, that ain't my character. It hurt to hear her tell me to leave, even though there wasn't any love left between us. I was only there for the kids. So yeah, it hurt, but I didn't show it. I just got my things, loaded up my truck, and walked out. I dropped my things off at my mother's, told her about the argument between me and D'marie, then went on into work at the club.

D'marie felt like I was disrespecting myself by working as a bouncer at my guy's nightclub. But that was far from the case. Yeah, to a small-minded individual like her, it looked that way. But when you're on the come-up the way I was, it was a stepping stone toward achieving my goals. Working those parties and clubs allowed me to network with people who owned all types of businesses. Truth be told, I enjoyed being a bouncer. I'm a nice size—five foot eleven, two hundred and twenty-five pounds solid, with a pretty violent background. On top of me being big and midnight-black, I'm pretty intimidating. And almost daily, I do basic self-defense conditioning as part of my exercises to stay in shape.

Anyways, that night I should have found something else to do or just stayed at my mom's place, because whatever was in the air that had D'marie trippin' also had the city going crazy. Like an hour or so after I'd gotten to work at *Club Embassy*, some *No Love* guys who were all drunk and acting wild got into a heated argument with a clique off of 33rd Street. I didn't have time to intervene. By the time I made it to them from my post at the entrance, fists had already been thrown, kicking off a good ol' bar fight.

I ran up and tossed a couple of drunk *No Love* boys away from a group of females they were being overly aggressive with. I guess their big homie didn't like me treating his guys the way I had because he rushed me from behind. He would've got me had I not caught a glimpse of his reflection in the large mirrors surrounding the dance floor. Before he could hit me with the angry haymaker he had cocked back for me, I spun around and kicked him hard in the chest. He went crashing backward into some of his other guys. Some other guy came at me from the left with a bottle. I sidestepped real fast, at the same time as the other bouncer grabbed ahold of his wrist and yanked the bottle out of the surprised fool's hand. I hit the punk with a hard hammer fist that made him take a knee. I didn't stop at that, though. I pounded his face a few more times, bloodying it. I only stopped because his big homie pressed the barrel of his gun to the back of my head. Glancing in the mirror, I saw that we weren't that far away from the stairs. Being the true street nigga that I am, I didn't panic. I carefully put my hands up in surrender, praying it would make him feel more in control.

"C'mon, man, ain't no need fo' all of that. I'm just doing my job," I said, slowly backing him towards the edge of the stairs.

"Fuck a job! It's *No Love*, nigg—"

Before he could finish his statement, I abruptly dropped down, pushing him backwards while simultaneously reaching up and grabbing his gun hand. I slammed it down onto my shoulder hard, causing him to release his grip on the gun as he fell down the stairs. The gun skidded across the dance floor, where some corner store wigged thot had the audacity to kick it right back towards him. One of his guys quickly picked it up and took aim at me before I could get to it. I couldn't believe that punk-ass broad had done that shit.

"Man, ain't no need for no gunplay. I'm just doing my job," I pleaded while looking for help from the other bouncer working with me. I didn't know where Bear had vanished to. I knew he wouldn't leave me hanging, but I didn't know where he went.

One of the hood bosses stepped up and ordered them to put the guns away while holding them at gunpoint.

"Big Boi, I'm out here tryna have a good time tonight, and you muthafuckas are fuckin' up my night on some out-of-pocket drunk shit!" said the short, cocky gangster with a mouthful of gold and like over fifty thousand bucks worth of icy jewelry draped around his neck and wrists.

I'd seen him and his clique in the club pretty much every night since I started working there. I knew he was tight with my guy, the owner, and that everyone called him Lil Buddy. I also knew that the two goons who were always with him were called Fat Tone and Cuzo. I was so glad that Bear had gone and got them to step in because I wasn't strapped, and this wasn't no TV shit. No matter how good I am with my hands, I was not going to make it against a group of guys all mad at me with guns.

"Now, my niggas here is just doing their jobs so we can keep havin' a good time in this bitch." Lil Buddy nodded my way, and I returned the nod. Then he continued by telling them that if they had an issue with me, then they had an issue with him that they needed to address.

"Naw, it ain't nothin' with us, Lil Buddy. Fam, we good. I'll catch this clown-ass nigga in the streets," Big Boi replied, staring me down with the meanest mug he could make. I chuckled, holding my tongue, because we both knew he doesn't have a winning chance with me one-on-one, or any other way without weapons being involved.

"Alright, everybody, that's it for the night!" DJ Tone announced over the sound system and received boos from the crowd. "Don't boo me. This is all thanks to the fools who couldn't act right in here tonight. Now we gotta call it a night, but we'll be looking forward to seeing all of the grown and sexy back here tomorrow . . . Let's give it up for Bear and AR, to let 'em know that we all feel much safer now that they're on the job."

With that said, Bear and I got the club cleared. I collected my pay, then left the owner and his friends to their little private after-party. I called it a night and went home to my mom's crib.

Chapter 8

Mica and her sister both nursed slight hangovers the day after they had liberated her from her abusive ex. Before the police car's tail lights had fully disappeared off the block, the wildhearted sisters had a bottle of Patron cracked open in celebration of their accomplishment. While drinking and cleaning up the mess they made, they went around the house packing all of the punk's things into big trash bags.

Now, after Mica took her sister home, she sat alone in her bedroom, going through a mental checklist of all of BG's belongings. She needed to make sure that they had packed everything because once his sister came and got his stuff, she didn't want him coming back around for any reason. That relationship was done, done! In a momentary flood of emotion, Mica dropped down, her arms wrapped tightly around her knees, and released a big, cleansing cry. Even though she was happy her sister had talked her into doing what they had done to free her from the abusive, loveless relationship, Mica hadn't done anything so frighteningly impulsive in all her twenty-nine years of life. Exhaling the last of her pain, she sprang to her feet. Walking with the quickness of a tweaking crackhead, Mica gathered the trash bags two at a time and hauled them out to the front porch, where she left them to be picked up. Then she freshened up and went to get her kids from her mother.

* * *

The evening after all the craziness at the club, I was out running around doing some drops and cash collecting before I headed down to the Illinois car auction for the second time since I'd made the decision to pick up another dope sack. I really felt like selling used cars was my thing. If nothing else, it was worth me exploring the legitimate hustle further. On my first trip, I copped six cars and sold them all within a few days, almost tripling my investment. So this time around, I wanted a nice-sized inventory to work with so I could really see how it fits me.

Twenty-fo's on yo' car, you's a trap star / If you known to buy the bar, you's a trap star / You got ice around yo' neck, you's a trap star . . .

I was in my Chevy Tahoe, slammin' Gucci Mane's song "Trap Starz," cuttin' it on four fifteen-inch L-7 Kickers when I got a call from a young D-boy named Willie. I'd gotten cool with him working the aftersets after the club. Anyway, this turned out to be another time I should've followed my first mind and had him meet me at the casino, since it was right down the street from the highway. But nah, I was a hustler blindly chasing a goal. Being true to the code of the streets, when the money called, I went running.

Even if I wasn't on my way out of town, it would've been hard as hell for me to pass up dumpling 63 grams for two thousand two hundred and fifty dollars. The extras that I was looking to make off of it were right on time for my heading out to the auction. The reason I should've followed my first mind is because after meeting with Willie, I was walking back to my truck—reading a text from a friend of mine who calls herself my bar wife—not really paying attention to my surroundings when I got snatched up from behind.

Nigga done set me up, I immediately thought.

Then I heard, "Yeah, bitch-ass nigga, you thought you was gonna get away with that shit you did last night, didn't you?" the assailant growled in my ear while tightening his arm around my neck and chest.

41

I tried to get loose from him, but he had some other niggas with him who started hitting me with vicious punches, in rapid succession. I again tried to throw the first dude off of me, but he held on until I wildly spun and slammed him into a parked car. As soon as I broke away from him, I grabbed him by his funky-ass braids with one hand, and with the other, I punched him in the face. The force of my blow caused him to fold over at the waist. I kneed him in the face before letting him fall dazed to the ground. I quickly faced his guys. They were clearly shocked because they hesitated a moment too long. I jumped between them and went to feeding them a few hard and hateful fists and elbow combinations that knocked one out cold and sent the other one running back to the porch. I didn't wait to see what he was doing next. I immediately took off running through the nearest gangway between the houses across the street. I made it to the alley without being shot in the back. I didn't run far. I actually just ran around the house back to the front. I watched my assailants pile in a car and drive off, so I hurried up and got in my truck and sped off in the opposite direction.

In all of that bullshit, the three of them didn't do any real damage to me. Keeping it real with you, all I had was a little headache and a bloody lip. Hell, it wasn't enough to stop me from making it down to the car auction before the bidding started.

Chapter 9

Maybe a couple of weeks or so later, Mica had thoroughly finished sorting through any and all lingering emotions connected to her breakup. She truly felt an enormous sense of relief as she got herself dressed for work. Pleased with the way her jeans hugged her curves, she pulled on her top and sprayed her hair to give it that shine she liked. Mica had a few stops to make before going in to work her third-shift nursing job.

"I don't want Lita calling me back tonight talkin' 'bout y'all not listening to her!" she warned her sons as she slung her Adidas canvas work tote over her shoulder. "I'm not playin' with y'all hard-headed asses! Don't make me come back home!" Mica turned to her teenage cousin, Lita, who'd agreed to babysit for her in exchange for Mica doing her hair. "Lita, call me if you need to. Don't let 'em stay up too late playin' that game. They asses will stay up all night if you let 'em," she warned, then walked to the car.

The night air was heavy with moisture, promising a good rainfall as she quickly got in her car and answered her phone. Mica's good mood was instantly dampened when her car wouldn't start.

"Uggh!" she exclaimed while making hopeless attempts to get it started.

"Wassup, gurl?"

"I need a jump. This damn car won't start," she said to her cousin, whom she was on the phone with. Voice thick with frustration, Mica slammed her palm against the steering wheel, eyes narrowing as she glanced at the dashboard.

"Do you know what's wrong with it?"

"Yeah, it's the battery. The crazy thing is, I bought a new one the other day, but the man at the auto parts store said he couldn't put it in for me . . . Uggh! Why me!"

"Aye, why don't you go see if one of them old dudes that be fixing on cars down the alley from you can put it in for you?"

"I need it done now. It's dark and sprinkling rain; ain't nobody finna be down there workin' in this shit," Mica said, glaring out the windshield at the seemingly deserted, dark alley behind her.

"Just go see. If they ain't in there, then knock on the door. I doubt if they drunk asses will turn down making some quick, easy money," Shay pressed.

"Okay, bitch, if I get cussed the fuck out, you're paying for this."

* * *

In my haste to put distance between me and the guys that jumped me awhile back, I must've run over something or hit a pothole. I don't remember, but something destroyed one of my truck's flood lights. That night, I hit big at the auction though. I only picked up ten vehicles, but they were all in high demand, so I had to make time in my busy days to stop and pick up a new set of flood lights from AutoZone. It wasn't until I was down to my last car and the last bit of work that I had time to go out to the garage to do the repair.

My uncle Curt, who's also my business partner at the garage and used car sales business, had gone home for the night, so I worked on the lights alone. I enjoyed the quiet that the soft night rain cast over the rowdy neighborhood. Swapping out the floodlights had me really scrutinizing the events leading up to my attack. I can't lie, I was feeling some type of way.

So after handling my business at the auction, I, along with my little brother Ville and two of his goons, drove down on Wolly. When I confronted him about the attack, he was shocked to find out that it was me. He claimed that the girl in the house next door was the one who had told him about the attack that night. He just didn't put two and two together to know it was me that she was tellin' him about. In the end, I can't really say if I was set up or if them fools just so happened to be at the right place to try and get some vengeance.

I told Lil Buddy about the incident, and he told me not to trip on it; he would look into it. I didn't have any more issues after that.

Anyways, I had just finished wiring up the new floodlights when I heard a light, feminine voice from out of nowhere. I'd been so engrossed in the install that I didn't hear her approach.

"Excuse me!" she repeated louder the second time. I wasn't intentionally ignoring her; I just didn't think she was addressing me as sir. The only reason I rolled from under the truck was to be nosey.

When I rolled from underneath the front end of my Tahoe and stopped dead still, the beauty attached to the voice standing there made my blood rush a little. She had a nice body that wasn't anywhere close to balling her chubby, nor angular. She stood maybe five-foot-three or so. I couldn't really tell because I was looking at her from the ground up. Put it like this: she had the body of a hip-hop magazine model. She was dressed in tight-fitting Coogi jeans and a matching baby blue and pink hoodie.

"Wud up?" I replied as coolly as I could.

When she shoved the mess of long, wavy jet-black braids behind her ear, drawing my eyes from her thighs up to her face, only then did I recognize her. She was the mother of the kid I'd rescued. My instant thought was that she'd seen me down in the garage alone and came to finally say thanks, but the expression on her face told me she wasn't expecting to see me. I watched her take a quick mental survey of me and the garage.

"Is this your garage?"

"Yeah, why?" I replied, at the same time scanning the dark alley behind her in case it was another set-up or ambush. I wasn't getting caught . . .

"Umm, can you help me? My car won't start."

"What's wrong with it?"

"It's the battery. I need it put in or a jump start, either one. I just need it done now because I gotta go to work tonight."

"Sure, I can do that for you right quick," I agreed, liking her intelligent, deep brown eyes. "Where's your car?" I inquired, while, as discreetly as I could, easing the .357 automatic handgun that I had under the truck with me into my back pocket as I stood up.

"It's right at the end of my driveway," she pointed down the alley toward her house.

"So you want me to follow you down this dark-ass alley?"

"You don't gotta be scared. I'm not on nothin' but tryna get my car fixed," she pushed her hair behind her ear again and flashed a sexy, teasing smile.

"I'm not worried, just lead the way." I fell in step with her, checking her butt out the whole way there. When we reached her driveway, it confirmed that I was right—she is the mother of the boy that got hit by the truck a couple of months ago. I started to bring it up but then decided not to make things awkward and just fix the car. "Does it start, or do I gotta push it?"

"Nope, not without a jump," she replied, standing beside her black Chrysler 300M. "You look strong; you can push while I steer it," she smiled again.

"Why do you get the easy part? How about we both push it?" I joked.

"I can't move that big-ass car!"

"I'm joking. I just wanted to see your face. Just get in and steer. I don't understand why your pretty ass don't have a light in this damn driveway," I said, regretting not grabbing my booster box.

"I said the same damn thing the other day. The girl upstairs from me said it used to be one out here, but some crackhead stole it."

"Them damn crackheads," I said as the car coasted down the slight-sloped alley. Once at the garage, I maneuvered the nose of the car out of the drizzling rain so I could work on it.

"I hope you can do it. The worker at AutoZone couldn't do it because he didn't know where it is."

"How in the fuck don't he know where it is, when he works at an auto parts store? It's his job to know where it is," I shook my head. "He lied to you, Ms. Lady. He just didn't wanna take all of the stuff off that he has to in order to get to it," I explained, pulling out a small flashlight and showing her exactly where the battery was under the hood.

"I see it. Wow, it looks hard to get to. Can you do it? I mean, do you really know what you're doing?" She had this serious, really skeptical look on her face that made me smile.

"What, now you don't trust me to do it? Wow! You made me push this damn car down the alley in the rain only to have second thoughts now?"

"No, it's not like that . . . You just don't look like you work on cars for real, that's all. I didn't mean anything by it."

"What do you think I was doing when you walked up? Whatever, I can hear the skepticism in yo' voice. It's all good though," I walked over to the toolbox and gathered the tools I needed to do the job. "You can step on in here outta the rain so you can be dry while you watch me work."

"Are you mad?"

"Not even close . . . Where's the battery?" I inquired, then started unhooking stuff to get the old battery out.

"It's on the floor in the backseat," she answered, then went to talking softly on her phone, which she had been holding an open line on the entire time since she'd hooked with me. I guess it was kind of a safety precaution in case I did something to her. If anything were to happen, the person on the other end would call the police—smart move.

It only took me a few minutes to put the new battery in and get the car started for her.

"All done," I announced, spreading my arms like a magician to show her that everything was back in its place.

"How much do I owe you?"

"You know what, just buy me lunch."

"Lunch, are you sure? I'll do that too, but I can pay you."

"I'm not insinuating that you can't pay me. I'm just being a friendly neighbor. You can pay me by thinking of me first when you decide to buy another car. I also buy, sell, and repair cars. So your payment is keeping me in mind when you or your friends are looking for a nice, affordable used car."

"Okay, I can do that. Do you have a card? What's your name?"

"My name is Assa, you can call me AR if it's easier to remember." I flashed a friendly smile. "I don't have a card, but you can have my number." I gave her my phone number, and she stored it in her phone.

"Your wife ain't gonna trip on me calling you, is she?" she asked, letting me know that she'd noticed the ring on my finger.

"Not unless you call me for something other than the things I told you that I have to offer." I saw the hint of disappointment in her eyes at my response, so I tried to clean it up. "No, seriously, I don't have that issue anymore. I just wear the ring outta habit."

"Is that right?"

"Yeah, it is. But I know I don't have to worry. I mean, think about getting a call from you about anything other than that, because yo' man won't let that happen."

"Yeah, right!" she chuckled. "If I had a man, I wouldn't be down here stuck in the fuckin' rain by myself."

"Man, boyfriend, whateva you call him, I know better than to believe you don't have one. I've seen y'all together, that day when your lil' boy almost got me killed."

"Wait, what? . . . Oh my God! That was you?"

"Yeap, it was." Right then, my phone beeped, letting me know I had a text. I quickly scanned it. It was from one of the bros trying to re-up with me before it got too late. I don't know how many times I've told everybody that it is never too late to call me when it's about money. Day or night, rain or shine, I'm coming to get it. "I'll be looking for your call. It's time for me to get to my other job."

"Wait, you can't just tell me that you're the one who saved my son's life and run off."

"Don't worry about it. Just call me when you can," I said, then went to preparing to finish up the repair on my truck so I could go.

"Whatever, you know that was your wife. She probably see you out here talkin' to me and told you to come in the house," she said real sassy-like.

"First, I don't know how to put a battery in a car, now I'm a liar? Stop pickin'. This is my mother's house. So that's the woman that you may have seen peeking out the window. Let's not forget 'bout yo' man, whatever he is. So why are you worried about my soon-to-be ex-wife anyway?"

"I'm not with that guy anymore, so I'm just weighing my chances of gettin' to know you better," she flirted before getting in her car.

"I'll be lookin' for your call soon," I said, then got back under my truck to finish what I started. She tapped the horn, then drove away. Shortly afterward, my phone beeped again. This time, it was Mica telling me her name's Mica and that I should save her number.

Chapter 10

Not wanting to continue making the moment awkward, Mica reluctantly walked to her car. I'd generated a small flow of dangerous emotions in her that she didn't have the time to act on.

"Gurly, I don't know who you seen working in that garage, but that was not an ole drunk. That nigga's fine!" She corrected her cousin, who told her about us alley mechanics.

"What's he like?"

"Umm, he's dark-skinned, with a neatly full tapered beard, a nice, sensuous mouth with them kissable lips. He's tall, about six feet or somethin' like that. He has on a long-sleeved black tee that looked like it was tailor-made to fit his broad chest and shoulders."

After we got together, Mica admitted to me that she'd slipped into a brief daydream of me shirtless, pulling her into my arms.

"Mica?" Shay knew her cousin was really feeling me because of the way she was going on and babbling about me.

"Huh?" she snapped out of her thoughts.

"Don't forget I was on the phone the whole time, so I heard everything you're telling me myself. Nah, bitch, shut up and text him your number right now. You know if he calls you right away, that he's feeling you too."

Mica did what Shay told her to do, then headed on into her third-shift job with a little smile on her face from receiving my immediate response.

*   *   *

The overall atmosphere at work was busy—really *busy*—with Mica working a bit of overtime, training a new girl, as well as dealing with the challenges of having not one, but two new uneasy clients. The only good thing about her work situation was that the new girl was hardworking and willing to pitch in with all of the clients in whatever way she could.

Surprisingly, after putting in just about twelve hours at work, Mica wasn't ready to go home to her bed just yet. So, she decided to drop in on one of her close friends. Stepping out to her car, Mica instantly noticed the pollen in the morning air because her allergies had kicked up. She got in the car and thought of me when it started up without the slightest hesitation. Mica felt a little tingle down low, deep in her loins from her thoughts of me as she pulled away. She knew her friend Jazz was always up for some juicy gossip and ready to spill the tea about somebody's business. Which is why Mica believed Jazz was just the person for her to ask for thoughts on how she should approach getting to know me better. Hell, getting to know me ain't ever a hard thing for a fine-ass woman like her. All she had to do was call me over and let nature do the rest.

Anyway, she made it to her friend's house, got out, and rang the doorbell just as her allergies kicked up. Mica was teary-eyed from fighting not to release another round of sneezing. As soon as Jazz opened the door a crack, she pushed her way inside.

"Hey, gurl, let me in this house," she said, right then losing the battle with the sneezing fit.

"Whoa, whoa, hey!" Jazz stammered, quickly glancing from her friend to the bedroom door.

"Whoa, nothing, gurl. I need some tissue. These damn allergies of mine are kickin' my ass this morning," Mica explained, while noticing how Jazz's eyes kept anxiously rolling from her to the slightly closed bedroom door. "What, am I interrupting somethin', gud-gud?" she inquired with a naughty smile. Jazz was about to answer when she spotted the shadow of her guest moving toward the door.

"Aye, hold up . . . wait!" she shouted nervously, rushing to grab the doorknob. But she wasn't fast enough. Stepping out of her bedroom half-dressed came Mica's nightmare, BG.

"Jazzy, can I use your car to make a—" the punk's words got hung up in his throat when his eyes fell on Mica.

"What the—" Mica's mouth fell open in surprise, which quickly turned into extreme agitation directed at both of them.

"Mica, it's not how it looks. Let me explain," Jazz petitioned.

"Let you explain what? Huh, bitch? Explain what?" Mica shouted as she backed away from the two of them and toward the exit. "I can't fuckin' believe you! After all of the times I've come crying to you about how that nigga was beating my ass and fuckin' off on me, and you got him here! I should've known yo' disloyal triflin' ass better. Bitch, I bet it's been you that he's been fuckin' this whole time. I thought you was my friend!" Mica rushed out of the house quickly, putting some distance between herself and BG before he decided it was a good time for some retaliation.

"Mica, wait it—"

"Save it, bitch! I hope y'all die together! Don't fuckin' call me when he get to beating yo' ass next . . . Dumb bitch!" Mica shouted, got in her car, and sped away.

Tears stung Mica's eyes from the crazy wave of emotion that had her head pounding as she sped home. Out of nowhere, she spotted flashing police lights in her rearview mirror. She swore out loud, knowing that they were coming for her because of her speeding. As soon as the police car caught up to her, she pulled over and stopped. Knowing how trigger-happy police could be, Mica placed both her hands on the top of the steering wheel in plain view and waited for the officer to knock on her window. When that first knock came, so did a new wave of tears, followed by her lowering the window.

"Do you have any idea how fast you were going in this school zone?" the officer questioned.

"I'm sorry, officer. I just ran into my abusive ex-boyfriend and was trying to get away from him before he could hurt me again," she answered, letting the tears fall freely.

"You know what, I believe you," he said, taking a closer look at her. "Are you hurt in any way?"

"No. He didn't touch me, but I just had him put in jail for hitting me, so I know he's mad at me."

"Ma'am, is there a no-contact order in place?"

"Yeah." Mica's voice was thick with emotion, but her mind was elsewhere, replaying the confrontation over and over. Her heart was racing, her thoughts scattered. All she wanted was peace, but that damn ex—and the betrayal—was still in her head. She exhaled slowly, trying to gather herself.

"Okay just to make me feel better I'm going to follow you to your destination to ensure that you get there safety. Is that alright with you?"

"Yes. Thank you!" Mica exhaled in relief, thankful that an Angel was looking out for her with the way her day's starting out.

Chapter 11

If things went the way I'd planned then, I would've had my car lot up and running and in a few months I would've been on my way to being legally financially independent. I've been a block bleeder pretty much all of my life. I was tired of looking over my shoulder for them dirty alphabet boys to come round me up again. It seemed like every damn time I got up in the game I got locked down, thrown in one cage or another. This time my plan is to invest in myself and get established in the world the legal way.

With that on mind I continued working at the club, but to make sure that I was taken more seriously, I went out and bought a few needed accessories. Like a heavy black steel retractable baton, a nice shiny security shield that I hung on a chain around my neck. I put all of it on with my signature black T-shirt and Dickie cargo pants and went to work.

The night was smooth and uneventful which is always a good thing. While making my rounds of the parking lot I spotted a black car that made me think of Mica. I don't know, there was something about that woman that had me truly attracted to her. I found random thoughts of her coming to mind more and more. I fought the urge to call her I needed to stay focus, plus D'marie was still on something with me.

Hell, that night I was chillin with a female that I'd been fooling around with here and there, off and on, when D'marie's friends entered the club and seen us they immediately called her and she flew her ass down to the club. As soon as I spotted my soon-to-be ex-wife enter the club, I told my friend who she is just in case D'marie decided to get on some bullshit. As the night got going, the crowd got drunker and wilder. I had to leave my friend to assist the other bouncer with a small issue at the door, so I didn't see D'marie go and start fuckin' with her. The next thing I know, ol' girl was stomping out of the place, telling me to call her when I got my shit together. I was just standing there wondering what had happened when D'marie came over to me, talking shit.

"I see yo' ugly ass bitch ran off." She was clearly tipsy.

"Dee, grow the fuck up. You don't see me trippin' about that lil bitch boy you were back there with that had his hands all over yo' ass and shit, so gon' wit' that!"

I saw the smile in her eye and knew what I said made me sound jealous, so I turned my back on her and busied myself with checking ID cards at the door.

After forcing myself to ignore D'marie for a few minutes, I took a glance over my shoulder and spotted her sitting at the bar, glaring at me. From the look in her eyes, I could see that the laughter was gone. Now they showed that she was hurt. Let's not forget that she asked for this — I'm only respecting her wishes. I thought about telling her to go home, but everything about the way she was looking at me said that she would make a scene, and I didn't want that, so I left her be.

Last call came fast — just the way I needed it to. I'd busied myself so much that I didn't know that she had left the club. All I know is, when I got to clearing the place, she was nowhere in sight. I thought I was good, but I thought wrong.

When I pulled up to my crib, I right away noticed her SUV parked at the corner. I'd bought the damn truck for her, so I knew the thing anywhere. By the time I parked and stepped out of my truck, D'marie had pulled up and stopped right behind me with the window down.

"Can we talk?" she asked, crying real tears.

"What do you want? What is it to talk about? It's been months. Now that you see me with someone else, you got time for me? I'm good."

"What about our family and the kids?"

"You did this. Let's not forget that. So don't try to make it seem like it's me," I retorted, shaking my head in frustration and feeling kind of embarrassed by the whole situation.

I ended up allowing her to plead her case. She said something about not wanting to look weak to everybody. I didn't understand any of that shit. What I did understand is, she wasn't worried about me until she saw me with someone else. I reminded her of her actions that got us where we are in our marriage, then I went in the house. This time, I did tell her to take her ass home.

Chapter 12

After that messiness when Mica discovered her friend's betrayal, and that BS my ex-wife had pulled with me later that same day, all kinds of mixed emotions played with our mental states. I guess you can say a kind of depression had fallen over the both of us.

For Mica, her state of mind had her shutting down and falling back from almost everyone except her mother, sisters, and cousin Shay — all of whom were just as pissed off as she was about Jazz and BG. After that day, all Mica did was work, come home and do her motherly duties, then lay in bed emotionally exhausted, wondering what she'd done wrong to deserve such a sad life.

For me, emotionally, I guess you can say it was pretty much the same way as for Mica. But instead of me pulling back from everyone, I fell deeper into the street life and got to hustling harder.

During this time, a lot of weird things started happening — like the sudden raid of my spots. Which was weird, because that trap house was fairly new, and no small bags of dope was being sold out of it. I mean it when I tell you there was almost no traffic coming in and out of the place for it to catch the eye of the law. So the only possible way the place got raided was for someone to put them people onto it.

The raid took place midday, shortly after I'd arrived back from picking up my re-up pack in Chi. The only thing that happened that day differently was I'd left my partner there to finish getting the orders together by himself because I had to go pick up my car from the shop.

I had gotten my 1984 Chevy Monte Carlo fully customized. I got it painted red and orange, which are two of me and my daughter's colors. The interior was done in the same colors, with matching backgrounds in the rims. Now everyone who knows me knows that I love combat sports, so it wasn't much of a surprise that I put the word *TAPOUT*, in those same colors, across the back window. Yeah, that car was my baby.

Anyways, I was just coming back from picking the car up when I got a call from D'marie. She sounded all panicked, questioning me about my whereabouts. My immediate thought was something was wrong with one of the kids, because there was no other reason for her to be calling me.

"I'm just picking up my car from Frank's. Why, what's wrong?"

"The police just called me asking about a light blue Maxima parked at a house they raided on 18th Street. Do you know anything about it?"

"Why did they call you?" I asked, making a quick U-turn and storming down Capital Drive towards the spot. "I need to find out what's going on with my niggah."

"I'm pullin' up there right now. Bae, I think these the feds. It's a bunch of black trucks out here."

"Why in the fuck would you go down there before talkin' to me?" I questioned, a bit more suspicious now.

"I'm supposed to come talk to a detective when I get here. He said I wasn't in trouble, that he just wanna know about the car. So what do you want me to do?"

Because she said she had to meet a detective and not an agent, I knew it wasn't the feds. Thinking quickly, I told her the car was hers and it was supposed to be a surprise for her birthday. That made her happy, taking whatever her thoughts about being mad at me and messing me over away.

I then told her to try to find out as much as she could about what happened so I wouldn't be in the dark when I got there. She agreed and ended the call to talk to the detective.

Not long after, I was parking behind her truck. I got out, spotting D'marie talking to a detective, and headed right over to them.

When he questioned me about the drugs, money, and guns that were found in the house, I played dumb, telling him that I'd parked the car there because the place belongs to a friend of mine.

"I don't know, nor is it my business, what the people who live downstairs do in their place. I've never met them."

This was all a lie, because I'd rented the whole house in one of my friendly hype's name.

The raid was a big hit to my pockets, but it almost hurt more to watch D'marie drive away with my car. I had plans for that car. I wanted to do something different for the car show in Elm's Grove.

It was better to have her spiteful ass smiling than not — especially at a time like that.

When it was all over and done at the spot with the police, I drove around in my Monte Carlo, running scenario after scenario through my mind about how the raid could've happened.

At that same time, I was trying to think of how I was gonna make a whole lot of shake in the midst of a drought. I knew the first thing I had to do was get a lawyer and bail money together for my partner as soon as possible.

Because when people feel abandoned, that's when they get to talking to them folks — and I couldn't afford that.

I was just heading to the garage to swap the car for my truck when I received a call from Mica asking me if I could come look at her car because it wouldn't start again. I agreed to come because I needed the distraction.

* * *

59

With her head pounding from stress and depression, Mica sat up in bed, rubbing her neck and shoulders. She was trying to relax some of the nagging tension that had been increasingly building up in her since she found out about Jazz and BG. Mica was seriously considering going back over to Jazz's crib and dragging her up and down the street for her betrayal. But Mica kept her children's well-being in mind. As long as she kept putting them first, she was able to not act on her vengeful thoughts.

When she couldn't stand the headache any longer, she got up, deciding to go get something for it. Since she hated taking pills, this meant she would have to leave the house, and no matter how bad she felt, Mica wasn't going to step foot out of the house looking a mess. So, she made her way into the bathroom, avoiding looking at herself in the mirror as she pulled aside the sky-blue floral printed shower curtain. She set the temperature, and when she had it just right, she stripped out of the pink Teddy Bear shirt and boy shorts that she wore to bed and stepped beneath the hot spray of massaging water.

Inhaling deeply as the water caressed her body, Mica's mind still wasn't at ease, but her thoughts had slowed. She exhaled slowly at the same time, tilting her head back so the water could massage her face. After about ten minutes under the spray, Mica was feeling a little relaxed. She stepped from the shower, wrapped herself in a towel, and ambled back to her bedroom, where she randomly dressed in teal and white striped sweatpants and a low-cut T-shirt that enhanced her full breasts. This time, she did glance in the mirror to be sure her ass was looking right in the pants.

"Lita, would you watch the boys for me while I run to the store? I need to get somethin' for this headache," Mica asked her cousin, who hadn't moved from her place on the sofa, watching TV and talking on her phone since Mica had made it home from work that morning.

"Yeah, bring me back some Flamin' Hots and a grape soda," Lita said, setting off a bunch of other requests from the kids.

Mica promised to bring them all something back, then walked out to her car, got in, and to her surprise, the car wouldn't start.

"What the fuck! You were just fine this morning, damn!" she complained to the car, dropping her head in frustration on the steering wheel.

I popped into her mind, and a small smile spread across her pretty face when she thought to use the car acting up as a reason to see me again. Mica called me over, explaining what was going on with the car, and I promised her I would be right over there.

A new excitement kicked up her mood from her anticipation of seeing me again. When she ended the call and raised her head to get out of the car, she found BG standing beside it, watching her.

"What the fuck!" she shouted, startled. "I don't got shit to say to you. Get the fuck away from me!" she snapped, her nostrils flaring in her anger.

"Who in the fuck do you think you talkin' to? Bitch, get outta the car. I ain't playing with you!" he barked as he snatched open the door and dragged her out by her arm. "I've been callin' and textin' you. How come you ain't hit me back?"

"BG, you're hurting my arm. Let me go and leave me alone," she whined.

"Make me leave you alone! You was bad when you and that bitch jumped me when I was drunk, remember? Where all that tough shit now?"

Mica didn't say another word; she just stared down at her feet, silently praying that he didn't beat her up again, as tears of fear fell from her eyes. Neither one of them noticed me coming into the yard. I didn't say anything at first. I just stood there, watching the light-skinned slim clown with these dusty-looking dreadlocks bark at Mica until I'd seen enough.

"Mica! Is he a problem?" Both of their heads whipped in my direction. They were surprised by my sudden appearance. A wave of intense emotion flowed across Mica's face. I watched her go from fear, to embarrassment, and then to anger. That's when she pulled away from him.

"Who the fuck is you?" this punk asked, putting his chest out like he's about drama.

"Somebody she knows . . . Mica, are you good?" I asked, a little more firmly.

"Naw, nigga, this ain't none of your business. Gon' 'bout yo' business 'til I'm finished talkin' to my bitch!" BG was annoyed by my intrusion but also fearful of me.

The dark backyard went silent and very tense for a moment as Mica looked from me to him, then back to me with pleading eyes. Her expression told me that she didn't want him there, and that was all I needed.

"Nigga, I don't know who yo' bitch is, but Mica ain't tryna fuck with you. So I suggest you leave," I said, moving closer to them.

"Okay, my nigga, you got it," he said with a clap of his hands in Mica's face. "Bitch, I'ma holla at you!" he threatened her, then briskly walked off into the darkness of the alley behind them.

The trouble was gone, and awkwardness, as thick as the moisture in the night's air, was left hanging between us. Knowing the embarrassment she felt because of the situation with her and her ex-boyfriend that I had walked into, I didn't even attempt to speak on it anymore. I just got right to work on her car. If there's something Mica wanted me to know about it, she would have to tell me on her own.

"What happens when you try to start it?" I inquired, breaking the silence as I walked over to her, standing beside the car.

"Huh, umm . . . It just keep tryna start, but it won't catch and start all the way up."

"Hmmm, get in and show me what you're talking about."

"Okay. It was running fine this whole time since you put the new battery in. I don't know why it started trippin' tonight," she explained, getting in the driver's seat and turning the key.

I could see the relief in her face that I didn't ask about BG, so I knew I was right not to bring it up. I just did my job, listening, trying to pinpoint the issue with the car by ear. I knew from listening that it wasn't an issue with the starter or the battery. Without thinking, I leaned inside the car to see if it was out of gas. It was almost a full tank, so I turned the key myself. It was then that I noticed that I was so close to her that I could smell her shower freshness.

Mica's scent was intoxicating. She moved in a way that she didn't mind our closeness. The way she positioned herself drew my eyes down to the black lace bra peeking from the low-cut neck of her shirt. My mind briefly slipped into a fantasy of me pulling her glossy lips to mine as I slipped my hand down her top, caressing her perky nipples. I inhaled softly and shook off the thoughts. Then I pulled the hood release, exhaling as I put some much-needed space between me and her fine self.

It took me about 30 minutes to figure out that her ex had sabotaged the car by removing the fuel pump fuse. Luckily, I just happened to have the fuse it needed in my tool bag. I popped it in, and the engine ignited happily when I turned the key.

Catching me completely off guard, Mica rewarded me for getting it started by leaping up into my arms. She locked her arms around my back, and her legs were around my waist in a tight, intimate embrace that made my blood rush. I returned the hug, all the while fighting the urge to kiss her. Instead, I put her down.

"Thank you so much for fixing it again for me. I don't know what I was gonna do if you couldn't figure out what was wrong with it," she thanked me, staring in my eyes and hitting me with that pretty smile of hers.

"To be honest with you, but not tryna be all up in your personal, I think you should seriously think of getting another car. Ol' boy is way too familiar with this one to sabotage it so easily. I…"

My phone beeped and vibrated in my pocket. I quickly read the text from one of my guys, then slipped it back in my pocket. "I gotta run. But call me later, though. It don't matter what time you call, I'ma be up. You can tell me how much you can afford to put on somethin' new, and I'll see what I can do for you."

"Okay. Something new sounds like a plan." She was smiling, but I could see a hint of disappointment on her face because I had to leave.

"If you have any other issues, please don't hesitate to call me," I told her as she walked me to my truck.

"Thank you for everything!"

I climbed in my Tahoe. If I didn't have to go address an issue at one of my spots, I had no doubt that I would've been making Ms. Mica cum for me. I waved at her as I pulled away, locking in my mind the way her sweatpants clung to her thighs.

Chapter 13

My night was crazy, *crazy* from the time I got that call from Mica's sexy self until I finally made it to the crib. I stayed on the phone with Mica until I heard her softly snoring. Everything just seemed so comfortable with her. During our conversation, we did touch on the subject of our ex's but didn't waste much time on the past. I agreed to find her a small SUV the next time I went to the auction. I planned to give it to her for her car and whatever cash she could come up with. I did that for young mothers. I was just trying to look out.

I told you that Ms. Mica has a sexy body, but I didn't tell you that she knows exactly how to use her sexiness to her advantage. I think me telling her to come up with as much cash as she could prompted her to make her next move.

It was a Friday night when Mica's friend Candi, who's an on-and-off-again exotic dancer, came to Mica asking her to come dance with her at a bachelor's party for a local rapper. The party promised her a big payout for her and another girl. The girl Candi had to go with her first backed out at the last minute, so she brought it to Mica.

"Gurl, fucking with these dudes, we're getting paid twelve hundred each just for showing up. Plus, we get tips on top of that."

"Twelve hundred and all I have to do is show up to dance?" Mica replied, knowing there was going to be more expected of her. This wasn't her first private party. Mica had done a few of them and more in her younger years.

By the time they made it to the hotel where the bachelor's party was being held, the place was already packed. The men had all types of bottles open, weed smoke in the air, and pills and powder on the table.

"Candi? Candi, we got y'all for the night, right?" The tipsy host asked as he handed her a wad of cash and gave her a soft tap.

"You got us for as long as your paper flows, Lil Daddy," she replied in a sexy, flirtatious tone of voice. Candi quickly glanced at Mica with a mischievous smirk on her lips.

"You bitches won't ever leave this bitch fuckin' with us!" another one of the guys joked, then pulled a big bankroll from his pocket and tossed it in the air above Mica's head.

"Is there a place where we can get ready?" Mica asked as Candi scooped up the cash.

By the time they re-emerged from getting dressed, Mica was tipsy off shots of Patron, and most of the guys were too intoxicated for much of anything. Mica allowed Candi to pull her sexy girl-on-girl strip tease for the crowd. Mica had it pretty easy because most of the guys there wanted a piece of Ms. Candi. It wasn't that she looked better, it was that the sound of her voice drove them wild.

Mica stayed close to the bachelor, knowing he wasn't going to push his limits too far from enjoying her lap dances. They both watched Candi doing her thing with the others. Somewhere between Mica making her ass clap and dropping it in the bachelor's lap, the others had lost half their clothes. Mica saw that Candi had done the same and was down on her knees, putting her mouth to work on one of the men. The little slut moved easily from deep-throating one guy to the next. While she was sucking and jerking off the two guys in front of her, a third guy was poking his fingers into her wet, hot hole.

Mica and the bachelor watched him increase the pace of his finger-fucking as well as the number of fingers that he was pushing inside Candi. When he had opened her up enough, he withdrew his fingers and eased his hardness in her in their place.

Mica stood in front of the horny bachelor, half-naked, watching him ogle her mouth-watering breasts and stiff nipples. She said, "What the hell," and fed them to him. The bachelor feverishly began licking and sucking on her dime-sized nipples. After a while, his mouth moved downward until his tongue was teasing her clit. Mica didn't stop him. She spread her legs nice and wide, allowing him to feast on her center the whole time imagining it was me. She closed her eyes, enjoying the pleasure up until the point that she felt an orgasm rising. Mica pushed him away from her, not allowing him the pleasure of making her cum so hard.

After she freed herself from his mouth, she reminded him that he was about to be a married man. She turned back to see how her friend was doing with the bunch. The four of them were still going strong. Candi was fucking and sucking with a look of pure delight on her face. Seeing that she didn't need any assistance, Mica went into the bathroom to get herself cleaned up and hide out until Candi was done. At the end of the night, Mica went home with a little over five thousand dollars. She planned to give four of it to me and spend the rest on her boys. But first, she needed a long, relaxing bath to wash away the night she had allowed her friend to talk her into.

It was almost two in the morning when Mica made it home, and everyone was just as they were supposed to be—asleep. She went straight into the bathroom and turned on the water to fill the tub. She left the water running, went into her bedroom, stripped, and gathered the things she needed for her bath, then returned to the bathroom. She felt a calmness as she savored the feeling of the running water as she adjusted the temperature. Once set, she peeled off her robe and stepped into the tub, easing her body into the steaming water.

Mica closed her eyes and sank back, savoring the feeling of the warmth covering her body. Having the bachelor's mouth on her at the party kicked up a yearning to be touched. She didn't just want to be touched by anybody, she wanted to feel my strong hands on her.

With thoughts of me on her mind, she cupped a handful of bubbles and rubbed them on herself. First, she ran her hands around her neck, massaging her shoulders. She smiled when she remembered her toy in the drawer. She quickly retrieved it and climbed back in the tub. Just the thought of its delightful vibrations sent tingles down her spine, and when she turned it on and put it where she needed it to be, that orgasm that she had held back earlier came splashing down.

Chapter 14

Zig-zagging through the city's blocks late Friday afternoon, I was lost in my thoughts, thinking about all of the craziness that's been going on around me. I usually would've been up bright and early in the morning, out checking my spots, but the loss of the 18th Street spot made me change things up. I'm really thinking that D'marie had a hand in it getting raided. The reason I believe she had something to do with it is because there was no reason for the police to call her about a car that has no attachment to her, other than belonging to her soon-to-be ex-husband. D'marie shouldn't have even known about that trap house's existence. Even if we're broken up, I wouldn't have put her name in the inner operations of my illegal business like that. So yeah, for me, the million-dollar question is: why did the police call her?

Then, the reason I had to rush away from Mica the other night was because I lost my South Side spot to an electrical fire. It's like the old saying goes, "When it rains, it pours." My only peace seemed to come from Mica, which was crazy because every time I'm around her, she has an issue for me to deal with. But I was really vibing with her. I found myself thinking of her more and more.

Mica works third shift, so we spent most of her shift talking on the phone while I handled my business in the streets. She wasn't aware of what I did for my money, outside of being a car salesman and a bouncer, nor did she question me on it. Everything about the woman says she's made for me.

While I was circling the ghetto, a homely-looking female with a delicious dark complexion and a nice butt stuffed in some skin-tight jeans caught my attention. She looked to be having some car trouble, so with cars being my thing, I pulled up on her and offered my assistance.

"What do you know about cars?" She was clearly annoyed and passing judgment because of my whip and the way I was dressed. "Uugghh, I don't got time for this."

"I make a living selling them, so I think I know enough." I clicked my hazard lights and got out of my van. "Get in and turn the key so I can see if it's something I can fix for you right quick." I instructed her as I reached under the hood, checking to see if the battery posts were tight. As soon as I heard that familiar clicking sound, I knew her starter was bad. "You need a new starter."

"Damn, not now!" she exclaimed, frustrated.

"I'm guessing somebody told you it was going bad already?"

"Yeah, my neighbor told me that it was going out yesterday when he got it started for me. Can you get it started so I can get home?"

"Not unless you have a new one in the car with you. I can have my uncle come tow it home for you."

"I don't have the money for that right now. I was praying this thing kept going until I got paid so I can get it fixed."

"You know what, this is your lucky day. I'mma have him tow you to the garage and see if he can rebuild it for you or put a used one on for you. If he can rebuild it, it'll be just like putting a new one on, but I can't give you a guarantee on the used one. You could get a year or just an hour out of it. It's up to you which one you want."

"All of it still sound way more than the sixty dollars that I got to my name right now."

"The tow is on me, but the beer for him to do the job is on you," I said, knowing I could use her help for something in the future.

"Really? You'll get my car fixed for some beer?" she said, genuinely surprised.

I placed the call for the tow, then while we sat in my van waiting on my uncle, we properly introduced ourselves to one another. She told me her name is Chrissy, but everyone calls her Muffin. When my uncle got the car hooked up, I followed him to the garage so she'd know I'm not trying to play her out of her car. My uncle said the job would take him a couple of hours to do because he needed to make a run before he could get started on it. Yeah, I could've taken over and got it done sooner, but I just didn't feel like getting that dirty.

Muffin asked me if I could take her home so she could put her groceries up while she waited for the car to be repaired. Because of how she was going about things, I knew she didn't have a man, or if she did, he wasn't available to her. Her cozy one-bedroom apartment confirmed that she lived alone. I asked if I could use her bathroom after I'd helped her get her groceries inside. I honestly had no intentions on fucking her that day. Maybe someday, but not that day. But when I came out of the bathroom, the next thing I knew, she was removing her clothes.

"Whoa, ma, wassup?"

"What's up is I'm tryna get some of that big black dick in my life. I ain't been fucked good in two months," she answered, tossing me a box of Magnums. "I have to give you somethin' for everything that you're doing for me." Just like that, she was naked on her leather sectional, on her hands and knees. And I was behind her, rubbing her clit with the tip of my hardness. I teased her with the tip until she was panting for me to put it in her. Then she reached back and put my length where she wanted it. I grabbed her hips and rammed all of me in her. Muffin cried out in ecstasy as I was pounding into her nice and hard. So hard that she had to brace herself from falling off the couch. Her ear-piercing moans of pleasure filled the small apartment. Muffin was so wet that when she got to throwing it back at me, I had to flip her over. I locked her knees under my arms and went right back in. In no time, it felt like a dam had been broken. When she came, I came right behind her and collapsed on top of her.

This was nuts because, at the time, nothing was even close to being said that Mica and I were even going to see if we were going to be together. Feeling the way I felt for a woman I hadn't even taken out on a date was crazy for me. I didn't even think twice when I was fucking off on D'marie. I told myself right then and there that I was going to get my hustle back together and then shoot my shot at Mica.

Chapter 15

Following our little fuck fest, Muffin's thot ass turned out to be more of an asset to me than I planned on making her. After making her cum like a waterfall once more for the road, she opened up, confessing to me that the reason she hadn't had sex in months is because she'd just gotten released from Milwaukee House of Corrections. She had caught a simple drug possession charge that landed her in the H.D.C. for five months. I just so happened to have seven pounds of good kush weed that somehow survived the raid. Since Muffin's hustle was weed and pills, I put two and two together. When I took her to pick up her car, I made a stop at my spot and put a couple of pounds in her hands to see what she could do with it.

Remember, at this time I was still in full grind mode, trying to bounce back from all I lost in the raid, then bailing my guys out of jail hit me up for almost sixty geez. That sixty that I didn't have to just give away, and then the South Side fire happened. In that fire, I only lost like two or three geez worth of work, which is nothing. The major loss was the house. That spot brought in a little over ten geez profit a day. So yeah, I fucked Muffin, a female I'd just met, because I needed all the help I could get, and so did she.

With Muffin off doing her thing with the weed I put in her hands, I ran to the crib and got myself cleaned up before hitting the streets again. I couldn't be out thuggin' smelling like her feminine body wash. Naw, I ain't have a girl that I had to worry about, but then again, I did have one that I didn't want to run off. All women give men sniff tests to see how we keep ourselves up. Anyways, I had just finished making a few runs when Muffin hit me up for two more pounds and my uncle called me, rushing me to get over to him with a quarter ounce of weed that he wanted for taking me up to the Fond Du Lac Auto Auction with him.

"Where you at, nephew? I'm tryna smoke before we ride out."

"I'm walking out now. I had to put together what you want," I answered while counting out the money I planned to spend at the auction. I locked the rest away in one of the two digital lockboxes that I kept stashed under the bed in the floor. Then I rushed out to my cherry red Ford Crown Victoria that I had sitting on twenty-two-inch Greed rims. I loved my Crown Vic because it was the first car that I sat on big rims back in 2008 when I got it.

After meeting up with Muffin and giving her what she requested, plus what was left of the pound I had dipped into for my uncle and sister, I stormed through the hoods heading to my uncle's crib on 28th Street. He was already sitting on the porch with one of his guys waiting when I pulled up. Unc rolled up a blunt, then tossed me the keys to his black-on-black Silverado that he'd already hooked the car dolly up to. The three of us hit the road, with me driving while they smoked and finished their beers. I made it to the auction house early enough for us to walk the lot and scope out the vehicles that we wanted most. I found two of the vehicles that I needed, including a midsize SUV that I hoped Mica would like. I made a list of other cars that I wanted, then went inside and found my uncle and his guy on the showroom floor.

Once the bidding started, the place was so loud that I could hardly understand what the fast-talking auctioneer was saying in the lane that I was in. The confusion for me was that there were three lanes going at the same time. I didn't take that into mind when I was making out my list. So yeah,

I missed out on the BMW SUV that I had scoped out for Mica, but snagged a nice two-door Ford Explorer with all of the bells and whistles that she'd told me she wanted. When it was all over, I had bought five cars, plus the Explorer. I found out that it was Jessie, my uncle's friend, who had outbid me for the BMW. I thought about trying to talk him out of it, but Mica had already said she liked the Explorer from the photos I sent her, so I left it at that. When I got the vehicles back to the garage, I immediately did my full inspection of the truck for Mica, then drove it down to her. She was genuinely pleased with it, and even more pleased with the price. I could've made close to eight thousand for it, but I gave it to her at cost, plus tax and title. So I made zero profit from it, but I made up for it with the sales of the rest of the cars I'd bought. A light, late snow had fallen, but nothing that stuck to the streets. I love the snow, so I was good with it. The temperature wasn't too cold or nothing.

"I'm outside," I announced when Mica answered the phone. I ended the call as I parked in front of her house. I got out and stood beside the Explorer, waiting to see her reaction. A few moments later, her door opened, and everyone came pouring out onto the porch to see the truck.

"Is that my mama's new truck?" the oldest of Mica's sons asked.

"Only if she likes it," I replied, smiling and enjoying the sight of her pretty smiling face as she approached me.

"Y'all get in the house, it's cold out here!" Mica exclaimed, sending her rightfully nosey boys and cousin back in the house. "Lita, take 'em in the house, they ain't got no shirts on and I don't got time to be dealing with no hard-headed sick kids."

"Sooo, what do you think now that you're seeing it in person?" I stared down into her sparkling eyes.

"It's so pretty!" she almost sang her praise as she slowly walked around inspecting the gleaming Explorer. "This is nice . . . I love it! But I don't think I can afford it unless you're willing to put me on a payment plan?"

"What do you mean you can't afford it? You pretty much own it already. Unless you want me to take it back?" I exclaimed, frowning at her in light confusion.

"Wait, you got this for me for the money I gave you? No way! Yeah, right."

"Actually, I paid less than that for it but rounded it off with tax and title. Oh, and I filled the tank up for you. So it's yours as soon as you sign on the dotted line," I explained with a small chuckle.

"Are you serious? Where do I sign?" Her excitement grew.

"Whoa. How are you just gonna sign for something when you don't know if it works? I could've pushed it down here for all you know. You haven't seen the inside." I lightheartedly scolded her, shaking my head. "Get in and take it for a ride." I handed her the keys.

"I don't—I never drove a truck before. I've always had cars." She shyly confessed while at the same time opening the door and peeking inside at the off-gray leather seats. She inhaled the fresh "New Car" fragrance that I hit it with before bringing it down to her.

"Whud . . . it got a sunroof! You didn't tell me it has a sunroof on the phone."

"I kinda did. I said it has everything you said you wanted. If you don't want me to take it back, then get in and drive the damn thing. It's no real difference than driving your car. It might even feel better for you because you'll have a better view of things on the roads." I explained, trying to encourage her.

"Mica, please make me understand how you want something you're scared of? That's crazy." She was at a loss for words.

"Come on, I'll go with you."

After driving cautiously for a while, Mica got comfortable and was whipping the truck like it was made for her. I had her take me to pick up my whip that I had left parked out front of my uncle's crib. Then she followed me back to the garage so she could sign the paperwork for her new purchased vehicle.

"I feel like I should give you somethin' for giving me this truck."

"I didn't give you anything. You paid for it, I just went and picked it out for you."

"You know what I meant." She rolled her eyes at me. "You should get somethin' for your time. How much would you have sold it for if it wasn't for me?"

"That don't matter because it is for you . . . If you want to pay me so badly, you still owe me food for fixing yo' car. Wassup with that?"

"Hmmm, what do you want to eat?"

I wanted to say "you," but instead, I asked her if I could have her next day off from work so I can take her out to eat. I told her that she could pay for it if it would make her feel better. She agreed, setting our date for that following Friday evening. Then my phone rang. My guy had sent me a text reminding me that he needed me to work at the club. So I was off to go get changed and go to work, and Mica was off to show off her new ride.

Chapter 16

Singing along with the songstress Marsha Ambrosius as she bellowed out her hit song "Late Nights & Early Mornings," Ms. Mica went through her normal morning chores as a working single mother without giving them much thought. She got on her boys about cleaning their bedrooms and taking out the trash while she cooked them a hot breakfast. Other than her nice SUV and the upcoming date with me, she really didn't have much new in her world.

Burning with anticipation, her mind kept drifting off to fairytale land. Mica went out and bought a new outfit and everything for our date. It was important to her that she showed me she's a good woman, especially after the incidents I'd witnessed between her and her loser ex-boyfriend. After showering and moisturizing her body, Mica hit herself lightly with some *Romantic Wish* perfume by *Victoria's Secret*. To be sure it gave her the effect she was looking for, she sprayed a hint between her thighs before dressing. Her short form fit her perfectly, making her ooze sex appeal. Mica took one last look in her full-length mirror hanging on the back of her bedroom door, then headed out.

* * *

My day pretty much started out the same as always. I got up, washed up, prayed, then dressed in my signature all-black hustling gear. I'm talking black T-shirt, black cargo pants, black shoes. The only brand that ever really changed on a daily basis is my shoes. I owned several black pairs. Anyways, I left her house in my Tahoe and went straight to McDonald's for my steak, egg, and cheese breakfast sandwich meal. Then I hit the streets, making my rounds and checking traps.

The one thing I'd learned for certain during my incarceration in the feds is that so many of us hustlers have access to things and people that could change our fortunes. The difference between being successful and unsuccessful, besides not getting caught, is self-confidence and keeping your eyes open so you can seize the opportunity when it presents itself. I'm very self-confident, which is why I move so low-profile that I was virtually nobody to everyone who did not know me prior to my eighty-four months of incarceration. I loved it. Because it not only allowed me to hustle inconspicuously, but it also made real bosses open up to me.

I also had to move the way I did because being a father, especially a single father, means that I have a helluva lot more to lose. My daughter is what changed up my routine for the day. She called me, asking me to bring her and her best friend McDonald's for lunch because she didn't like what the school was serving that day. You know I wanted to rack up some points so I could make her 'Daddy of the Year' list. I brought them what she requested. When I got to the school and saw my baby's face all bruised up with scratches on her cheek and neck, I snapped. She told me that her mother's husband tried to fight her and that she had to jump out of a moving car to get away from him. I don't know why her mother would allow that to happen, and I don't know why that nigga thought I would allow him to get away with it.

Because we were inside the school when the abuse was discovered, they called the police, so I had to follow all the legal protocols. I had to take my daughter down to the police station where they took photos of her bruises and our statements.

"You do not have to take your daughter back into an unsafe environment. You have the right to keep her with you," the officer explained after getting our statements. "Would you like to press charges?"

"All I want is my baby, and whatever paperwork I need to take her to court for this. From my understanding of the law, I don't have to press charges for y'all to do somethin' concerning child abuse," I stated. I had every intention of handling my business with the fool in the streets once I had my child secure.

I called my friend Dream, already on my way to her house. I asked if it was okay for my daughter to stay over there with her until I was done doing what I needed to handle.

"Of course, she can stay as long as you need me to keep her for you. You know I have an extra room now that Cassa is away at school," Dream agreed, then turned around and told me to go calm down and clear my head because I couldn't afford to make any dumb moves. She was right. So, after I got my daughter settled, I went home to clear my mind. My place was no place for a young teenage girl. She needed her own room, and my place was a studio apartment for the lifestyle I was living. It fit my needs. Speaking of needs, I needed to decompress, and my upcoming date with Mica was just what I needed to relax me some. I took my time and planned our date out. I thought she would be disappointed when I told her that I wasn't in the mood for large crowds, but to my surprise, she said she felt the same.

I tapped play on my 'Get It Wet' playlist, then strategically placed *Cherry Blossom* aromatherapy-scented candles around my bedroom. Being sure to double them around the bed so that the dancing light added to the seductive atmosphere, making my bed look inviting. Then I showered and dressed in a white with red and blue-trimming

Tommy Hilfiger polo shirt with matching blue slacks and shoes. I lightly tapped my favorite fragrance cologne by Usher, and waited for Mica's call. I didn't have to wait long before my phone buzzed with her text informing me she was pulling up. I rushed to the door, then tried to look as nonchalant as possible when I walked out to meet her at her truck.

She slid to a stop in front of me, and I walked around and opened her door for her. She smiled at me, letting her eyes roam over me for a hot moment before taking my hand and stepping out of the truck. The dress Mica had on looked like it was made just for her. I openly enjoyed her with my eyes, with every intention of peeling her out of her sexy outfit. I held her warm soft hand as I guided her inside the house. Mica asked herself how could I get better looking every time she saw me. She was impressed by my fashionable and expensive-looking outfit. Even more so by the time I'd taken to set the seductive atmosphere. She greeted me with a hug, inhaling and making a mental note that my cologne wasn't overpowering. My OG taught me at a young age that a little cologne goes a long way.

Standing there in the soft candlelit room with Maxwell's song 'Lifetime' playing in the background, Mica couldn't help melting a little as she stared up into my eyes. She wasn't alone in what she was feeling; I was right there with her. So much so that I skipped talking and kissed her sexy inviting lips. She allowed herself to fall fully into the kiss. I ran my hands down her butt. Mica is short, but her ass is so nice. We were so caught up in the lustful moment, I can't tell you who led who over to my bed. All I know is, I kissed almost every inch of her as I peeled off that dress. Then I scooped her off of her feet and gently lay her down in the center of the king-size bed, giving myself all of the room I needed to enjoy her.

From her reaction to my touch, I knew she'd never experienced anything so sensual from a true thug before. I started from the bottom, knowing it's the best way to work her up. I rubbed my thumbs along the bottom of her toes, massaging just above the ball of her tiny foot. Feeling my big, manly hands tenderly stroking that area ignited a lust in her that told me I had a full green light from there on. How it was about truly pleasing her, so I stood up and took off my shirt. Then I grabbed my bottle of creamy baby oil and climbed onto the bed with her. After slowly and sensuously stroking both feet, I dragged my hands up along the arch of her foot, leaving a silky sheen from the oil along the way. I was in no kind of rush, but from the way her hips rolled, she was getting desperate for me to bury my hardness in her deliciously moist center. I had her juices flowing before I reached her thick thighs. I love the way she felt as I moved up her body. I wanted so badly to slide deep inside her, but not yet.

My hands made their way to her butt. She arched her back, letting out a soft moan greeting my advances. She tried to slide more beneath me, so I got the message that she wanted me and needed me buried deep inside her. I used the little self-control I had to make love to her. At my touch, Mica soaked my bed way before I flipped her over onto her back and covered her lips with mine. I broke the kiss, guiding my hand in slow, firm, erotic strokes along the path between her thighs. When I penetrated her center, I saw her grab the sheets, fighting not to dig her pretty painted nails in my back and pull me in her. When I couldn't take it anymore, I stripped off the rest of my clothes and got face-to-face with her. Looking into her eyes as I pushed inside of her for the first time. The next thing I remember is her legs locking around me as we came as one.

Chapter 17

Here's some soft-ass shit that you'll never hear this thug say again. I've never experienced a love connection like the one I have with Mica, ever. The way we fit together is just magical. But all of that goodness that I was feeling came to a crashing halt. It wasn't because of anything Mica had done. No, no, no! It was because I answered the phone and agreed to meet up with D'marie.

D'marie called me all emotional, begging me to come talk to her, and being the sucka in that moment, I went. I went over there and ended up being arrested on a fake-ass domestic violence charge. She attacked me, but I was the one who got locked up behind it. That shit's crazy. So here's what happened! D'marie called me over to her house to talk.

"Bae, I know I was wrong. I love you and miss you. It's hard knowing that I messed up our families. I'm sorry. I'm begging you to forgive me and for you to give us another chance. I promise I'll be a better woman and a better wife."

"Dee, say all that shit when you're not fuckin' up and acting crazy, 'cause right now, it means nothing to me. I've risked my life, my freedom, and everything for you, only for you to shit on me. Move the fuck on, because I have." I snapped. "I shouldn't have come over here . . . don't got time for this," I exclaimed, then tried to leave. I said "*I tried to leave*," not that I left, because she jumped in front of the door. "We're done. Move!"

"No! No! You're not leavin' until I'm done talkin'!" she shouted, then got all crazy, pushing on me and shit. "Move me if you wanna leave, muthafucka! Move me," she screamed, grabbing me by my shirt and pulling me.

"Gurl, gone with that crazy shit. I'm not finna fight with you. You drunk," I barked, pulling away. She pulled back and ripped my shirt. "You're trippin'. Let me go!" I shouted, glaring at her, giving her full eye contact.

"You're not finna leave me so you can go be with them bitches! You got me fucked up if you think I'm finna let you just leave, nigga!"

"Whatever. Move!" I barked at her.

I only made her more angrier by provoking her. Because when I tried to go around her to get to the door, she went wild. She punched me in the face, just above my eye. I went to blocking her other hard wild blows and backing up away from her. That's when D'marie suddenly screamed and shoved me over the ottoman. Before I could get up, she went on to try to stomp on my head. I caught her foot and shoved her away from me. She stumbled over the coffee table, and I quickly got up. I saw that she dropped her phone, so I scooped it off of the floor, and then she tried to take it back. I tossed it across the room. When she ran to get it, I made my escape right out of the front door.

Her punk ass called the police, lying, telling them that I beat her up and all types of craziness that never happened. I ended up getting taken into custody and having to bail out of jail for like five hundred bucks for some mess I didn't do. I was given a month to appear in court for a domestic violence charge. Which was crazy because I'm the one who got beat up. They said because I admitted to pushing her off of me in order to leave the house, that was enough to charge me. That's crazy. What was I supposed to do, just let her stomp my head into the ground?

Then I appeared in that courtroom and saw that my lawyer and I were the only men in the room. I knew it was over for me. That was some 'Sisterhood' acting at its finest. The ADA came at us with an offer of 6 months of probation and ninety days of Domestic Violence counseling for my guilty plea. I didn't do shit to her, so no, I didn't accept that deal. I told them that I would plead no contest for the same deal, but not guilty. No contest means that I'm not admitting guilt, but I want to get things done and over with. The ADA agreed, but the judge didn't. The judge hit me with 30 days in jail, adding childcare privileges because she knew I had my daughter. A year probation, a no-contact order for D'marie, which I had no intention on ever going around her crazy ass again anyway. And lastly, I still had to do the DV counseling bullshit for ninety days.

Mica was highly upset and confessed everything. With her trust issues, it made it hard for her to believe that I wasn't still fucking my ex. The good thing was that Mica never believed that bullshit about me beating D'marie up. Her exact words were, "I've been with abusive niggas and you're not that." That made me feel good to hear her say because, keeping it a hunnid, that DV case did have me feeling a type of way. Anyway, I still had a few hours before I had to report to the jail to be logged in to do those 30 days with childcare. I also still had a few hours to do as I pleased, with the kids gone. I went to see Mica. Her cousin Lita let me in the house as she was on her way out, giving Mica and me the house to ourselves for a while. I found Mica in the bathroom. I knew Lita had sent her a text telling her that I was in the house before she took off, so everything I was witnessing was only done just for me. The bathroom door was slightly ajar, giving me a view of Mica's sexy nude body. I stood there watching as she stepped into the water of the tub. She glanced at me through the mirror, then eased her body into the foamy water.

"Bae, don't just stand there, come and wash my back for me," she said and closed her eyes, tilting her head back.

Without saying a word, I ambled over to the tub, grabbed the pink loofah, and swished it in the water. I sat on the edge of the tub, and she leaned forward, directing me to her back. I lightly dragged the loofah across her shoulders as my mind raced to format a plan to make her cum for me over and over. When I heard her inhale as she drew her knees to her chest, I leaned down, kissing her behind her ear, and she exhaled deeply, languishing in the intimacy of my kiss and the feel of my hands on her soft skin.

I teasingly inched my hands from her shoulders to her neck, then down to her breasts as I kissed her on her cheek.

Mica gasped, and her sweet lips parted, ready and waiting to accept mine. She leaned into my hands on her breasts as my fingers danced with her perky nipples. She suddenly reached up and grabbed the back of my smooth bald head, pulling my lips to hers in a lustful kiss. After a few hot moments, I broke away from her, stood up, and got undressed. Before allowing me to get in the tub with her, Mica pulled me to the edge of the tub and took my hardness into her mouth. She ran her warm tongue around the tip a few times, then sucked it between her soft lips. The feeling of her mouth work had me in another world. I hated to do it, but I stepped away from her before she got what she was working towards. I took a breath to center myself, then got in the water with her. I loved the feeling of her against me as I wrapped my legs around her. She leaned back, smiling up at me with her eyes closed and a glowing calm.

"Look at me," I ordered her, sliding my fingers down her stomach. She complied, but not before parting her knees for my fingers.

With her being so snug against me, I could feel the jolts of pleasure my touch was sending through her. I needed more room, so I got out of the bath, lifting her out with me. I placed her on the floor, and we kissed long and greedily before she leaped up, wrapped her short, thick legs around me, and began rolling her hips. I gave her what she was begging for. Cupping her butt, I lifted her and brought her down until I felt my tip part her center. I paused briefly to lock eyes with her, then completely drowned myself in her wetness. I set her on the bathroom countertop and commenced pounding her out until she was screaming my name and showering me with her love.

We did somehow make it into the bedroom, and by then, the only thing either of us had energy to do was cuddle up and talk until it was time for me to go and report to the jail. I wasn't trippin' on it like that because I only had to be locked up during school hours. I was supposed to be home with my daughter overnight. But that didn't happen. When I went in, the officer at the desk locked me up, talking some shit about they had to confirm my address before they could let me go again. So this is the kinda dumb shit the police got on with me. Remember, they have me in jail on childcare, with the understanding that I am a single father of a young teenage girl. They kept coming back to the holding cell, telling me that they went out to my address, and nobody was ever answering their calls.

I was in jail and my daughter was just out there lost, running the streets? I'm just kidding; she wasn't doing that, she was safe with my friend Dream, but the police didn't know that. They really didn't seem to care that my fourteen-year-old daughter was out there alone, possibly worried and scared about her dad. I'm glad I did not put that much faith in the system and had a backup plan.

Anyways, I missed my baby and my girl like crazy for the 30 days that I did in the Milwaukee County Jail. It was a hard thirty, too, because since I was supposed to just have walked in and back out right away, I'd left everything in my van with my cousin. I relied on my cellphone a bit too much because I didn't have any money to make a call with. I met a couple of guys in there who knew of me, but I didn't know anything about them. They were sympathetic about my situation. So they looked out, giving me hygiene and things like that to help me out. For their kindness, I promised to link up with them when I got out. They both were small-time hustlers trying to come up, and when I'm on the streets, I'm the one who could make it happen a bit faster for them.

But this wasn't my first time doing time in the county jail. I have a set routine that I fell right back into. I wish I could say playing dominoes and working out made the time go by fast for me, but it didn't. Like I said, I was really missing my daughter and girl, so it was the longest thirty days of my life. I was so excited when the officer came to escort me to the release staging. I was shocked when I was instructed to go to the cashier's window on my way out to pick up my money. I thought it was a mistake because I didn't have anything but the clothes I had on. I did as I was told and was given $20 cash and a check for $80. I didn't question where the money came from. I was just thankful for it. I happily thanked the cashier and hurried up and got the hell out of there before she caught on to the mistake.

I asked one of the guys I was released with if I could pay him $20 to take me to Mica's. I chose her place because I knew she would be awake at that time because she works third shift and could never really sleep through the night when she's off work. He agreed, and I gave him the cash. When I exited the building, I was met by my uncle Curt out there waiting on me. I let the guy I paid keep the money and went and got in with my uncle. I didn't care about the money, a mistake made by the county jail.

"Bastard, how come you ain't call nobody?" my uncle inquired in a scolding tone as I climbed into his van.

"I didn't have no money to call. I left everything in my van with Amo that day they locked me up, and you know I ain't begging a muthafucka for three-way calls and shit," I explained, smiling from ear to ear.

"What you mean didn't have no money? I put a bill on yo' books when Amo told me they kept you that day," he explained, pulling away from the jail.

"That's fucked up! Them muthafuckas didn't give me a receipt for it, so I never knew I had it. I just got it on my way out, and I thought the bitch fucked up and gave me some fee money." I noticed we were heading towards his crib. "Say

Unc, can you drop me off at Mica's? I'll have her take me to the house later."

"Shit, Bastard, you can drop yo'self off. I got yo' van parked at my house. I knew you were gonna need it ASAP when you got out because of all of the shit you got goin' on, plus I didn't want anything to happen to it with it just sitting outside of the house with nobody there for a month."

"That's good lookin' Unc. I knew somebody still loved me out here," I joked as he pulled up to his crib, parking behind my van.

Chapter 18

When Mica couldn't reach me on the phone at home for a few days, she went to the garage in search of me. When she asked if I was there, my uncle simply answered no. That sent her mind straight to negative thoughts. Had she inquired further, she would have found out that I had been taken into custody that same day that I had left her to report into the jail to start my child care. But no, my beauty's worry soon turned into heartbreak and finally into anger for allowing herself to fall for another man . . . so soon after getting out of a relationship—her thoughts went right to me getting back together with D'marie's punkass.

That same part of her mind knew deep down that wasn't true. Her mind refocused and set on my friend Dream. Since Dream was the one keeping my daughter for me, Mica's woman's intuition told her that it was once something more between me and the sexy vixen. Mica had convinced herself that I had left her to be with Dream, and the negative change in her mood didn't go unnoticed in her household.

After about thirty days of brokenheartedness, Mica decided that she was done moping around the house over me. Venting to her girlfriends about me, she allowed her cousins Star and Shimmer to talk her into attending their usual set girls' night with them. Mica's sister Kiyonnia came over to her house to get dressed and to keep my beauty from backing out on them.

Thinking that a whole lot of drinks was just what she needed to take her mind off of me, Mica did both of their hair, then got dressed in the most scantily clad outfit that she owned. Even though it was a spur-of-the-moment decision, her angry ass still put together a 'Come fuck me' outfit that would've gotten her in trouble with the last dude she was in a relationship with. Not with me, though, because my woman is my prize. Had I walked into a place and seen her dressed that way, I would happily enjoy the view because she would let everyone know who she's with as soon as she spotted me.

When you treat your woman the way she deserves to be treated, and not like a fucking hostage by feeding into those delusional trust issues, you don't gotta worry about her going nowhere because she's yours and she wants to be only yours.

"Sis, you know I live vicariously through y'all bitches. If you don't tell me nothing, then I never know the good shit," Kiyonnia spoke up over the music they were listening to on the way to the club.

"What are you gettin' at? 'Cause I include yo' nosey ass in everything," Mica replied as she made the turn off of North 27th Street onto Capital Drive.

"I'm curious, not nosey!" she retorted, rolling her eyes at her. "Okay, so tell me what's going on with you? One minute you were bouncing around bragging about AR, now you're all uuugghhhh!"

"Fuck him!" she exclaimed venomously. The mention of my name started a lust in her that she planned to try to forget that night. "He's out somewhere laid up enjoying himself, doin' him, and now I'ma do me," Mica stated with conviction as she was pulling onto Zeke's parking lot.

"How do you know that? He hasn't been to work at the club, and they've been asking about him."

"Hmmmmmmmm."

The sight before them had Mica cursing under her breath, looking for a place to park. Her cousins were right when they'd texted her and told her the place was packed. Mica so badly wanted to be on the main lot for two reasons. The first being she didn't want to park her truck on the street. And the second being it'd be closer to the entrance—or more so the exit after she'd gotten a little tipsy. Just as she was about to give up the search and wait, the perfect spot was vacated, and she quickly swooped into the space. Making short eye contact with the driver of the royal blue candy-painted 1996 Chevy Impala SS, rolling on 26-inch rims. The big chrome wheels made the car about just as high as Mica's Explorer.

Kiyonnia gave the passenger of the flashy car a flirtatious wave as they rode past them. Then self-consciously flipped down the visor mirror for the third time as Mica turned off the ignition.

"Kiyonnia, you're on point, gurl. Get outta the mirror and let's go. I need a drink!" Mica said, collecting her bag before they both got out of the truck.

Mica paused to straighten her skimpy purplish-red Dolce & Gabbana dress that she'd paired with gold Jimmy Choo thigh-high sandals. She could hear the hype sound of the song *Do It Bigger* by Lil Phat & Webbie blaring from inside the spot when a group of people exited. Mica looked up, and a guy fitting my description, standing beside the door across the dimly lit parking lot, caught her eye. Her liver quivered a little at the resemblance. The only reason she knew it wasn't me was because of his low brush cut. I'm big, black, and bald.

Still, seeing him added to her "fuck me" mind state. So this time, she was the one flirting with her eyes as they passed him and entered the club. Her cousin Wonda spotted them, and without alerting the others, she dramatically rushed over to Mica and Kiyonnia.

"Damn! It's about time y'all got here!" Wonda said, grabbing them by their hands and pulling them straight toward the dance floor.

"We been here, I just had to wait for a good place to park," Mica yelled over the music. "I'm not ready to dance yet. Let me get a couple of drinks in me first."

"Mica!" Like clockwork, Shay emerged from the crowd, saving Mica from Wonda. "Mica, come help me right quick," she stated, locking her arm in Mica's and smiling at Wonda and Kiyonnia as she pulled her away.

"Thank goodness you came when you did. I'ma need a whole lotta shots of Patron in me before I'm ready to be out there dancing—" Mica stopped in mid-sentence when she spotted my look-alike seated at the bar not far from where Shay was leading her.

"Is that the mysterious AR?" Shay inquired, following Mica's eyes to the man at the bar.

"I wish," Mica mumbled to herself. "No, but he's just as fine. A bitch might have to put his tongue to work at the end of the night. Make his fine ass a happy substitute," she replied, giggling and locking eyes with him for the second time.

"Oooh, you being bad tonight!" Shay sang, giggling with her.

"I'm not being bad, bitch. I'm single."

"He really just vanished on you. No calls, no nothing, just *poof*?"

"I'ma poof his ass when I see him! His ass better be dead 'cause I'ma kill 'im when I see him. I should've known better. The nigga's a used car salesman, be all nice and charismatic and shit, is how he be getting people to buy his cars." Mica vented, letting her thoughts rekindle her anger.

"Aye! Yo, bartender? Whatever she's is drinking, it's on me!" they heard the guy across the bar shout while smiling and pointing to Mica. He slapped a few bills on the bar. He raised his beer to her.

Mica winked, returned the smile, slammed the first shot, then walked away from the bar with her other shot. She intentionally gave him full view of her butt as she sashayed her way to the dance floor, where she joined the others dancing to Rae Sremmurd's song *'Come Get Her'*. Mica kept glancing back at him while she was bouncing and shaking her ass, just going hard as she could on the dance floor, having the time of her life. Did I tell you that her smoking cigarettes was the only thing I found wrong with her? She didn't smoke much, but it was still too much.

"What's good, Ma? I see you over here poppin' it for Money."

"Excuse me?" Mica turned around, finding herself face to face with the guy from the bar.

"They call me Money. I see you were poppin' that for me," he chuckled. "What's your name?"

"Mocha." Mica replied, letting a smile creep into the corners of her glossy lips and flipping her hair.

"Can we go outside and talk? I need a smoke break."

"That's fine, I could use one myself." She agreed, then glanced at her cousins, shooting them a shy wink before allowing herself to be led outside.

Exiting into the fresh night air, Mica allowed Money to take her hand and lead her around the middle of the parking lot, way past where she had parked. Noticing that they were moving away from the crowd, she suddenly became slightly uncomfortable. Mica wondered, did he think because he had bought her a couple of drinks, he was going to get between her legs? That question was quickly answered when he pushed her up against a car and stepped real close to her. Mica held up her hand, putting a stop to his moves.

"Wassup, Ma, why you wanna play?"

"This is not that. Thanks for the drinks, but I don't get down like this," she said, edging him back and moving away from between the cars so she could be seen.

"Babee, I didn't mean no disrespect. I'm not tryna bust you down here like some broke-ass nigga. We can go get us a room somewhere and chill all night."

Mica frowned, rolled her eyes, and released a loud sigh before she turned to leave. That's when he grabbed her dress to stop her. The thin, fancy fabric tore down the back, exposing her thong panties.

"Get yo' hands off me! Let me the fuck go!" she shouted at the top of her lungs, bringing attention to them. Money quickly threw his hands up, stepped away, apologized, and offered to pay for her outfit.

Zeke's parking security rushed over to see what the fuss was about and spotted her ripped dress and Money looking all panicky, shoving a wad of bills at Mica. The bouncer snatched the money from him, made him leave the club, then escorted Mica back inside the building, handing her the cash. Mica told the others what happened, then went home feeling worse than she had before she went out.

Chapter 19

We don't wanna / We don't wanna / We don't wanna neva end / We don't wanna / We don't wanna neva end . . .

"You got all the questions, I know all the answers. I took your heart, girl . . ." I sang along to Future's song *Neva End*, allowing the hard bass from the four 15-inch Sony CVX subwoofers to announce my arrival. I pulled into a park behind my beauty's Explorer, which was parked in front of the house just where I expected it to be.

Before I could get on the porch good, Mica had snatched open the door and leaped into my arms, giving me a hug and a kiss like I'd been gone for years. It wasn't until she got me behind the closed bedroom door that she questioned me about my whereabouts. I wanted to answer, but all I could focus on was her sexy self standing there in nothing but an oversized T-shirt. My kisses shut her right up, sending shivers through her that told me she wanted me as much as I did her. I kissed down her neck, sucking on her throat while I pulled the shirt off over her head. I stood back and stared at her, taking in her beauty, wondering just how much of our love exchange is actually true.

I snatched my shirt off, kicked off my shoes, and crawled over her until we were lying on the unmade bed. Then I dipped low, kissing her from her navel to her begging nipples. When I raced around the first one with my tongue, Mica gasped, so I immediately moved to the other, this time running my tongue slower around and sucking at the same time, which caused her back to arch and her to grip the back of my head. I don't know what took over me, but the level of intimacy that spilled from me that night had locked us in a zone that was much more than sex.

"I love you," she moaned softly when I pushed inside of her. Hearing her confession had me at a loss for words. I believed it was a fear of being hurt that held back my tongue. Instead of admitting that I was falling for her, I threw her knees up over my shoulders and gave her every inch of me.

Afterwards, as we lay, I fully explained what happened after I left her the day they had locked me up. I looked up and saw it was getting close for the kids to get up for school.

"I'm about to go so I can take Pooh to school. I wanna try to surprise her," I told Mica, smiling at the thought of seeing my daughter after being away from her for thirty days.

"And then what are you gonna do?"

"Come back here and take my black ass to sleep with you in my arms," I answered, covering her smile with my kiss before rolling out of the bed to freshen up some before I go see my baby.

We don't wanna / We don't wanna neva end / We don't wanna / We don't wanna neva end / You can leave today, I bet you comin' back tomorrow . . .

* * *

My daughter was just walking out of the house when I pulled up in front of her. She was so happy to see me that she started crying.

"Daddy!" she screamed at the top of her lungs as I got out of the van. She ran and leaped into my arms. I caught her and held my baby girl tightly. I'm not gonna sit here and tell you that I wasn't mad as hell behind that BS that took me away from her for thirty days. I had wanted D'marie to pay for that punk shit, so I cut her off right then and there. I didn't give her a penny. When she lied, I felt like she was saying not only *fuck* me but also *fuck* my daughter; so yeah, it was *fuck* her.

After I dropped my daughter off at school and promised to be there to pick her up when school was out, I went to the phone store and paid my bills so I could get back on my grind. As soon as I was back online, I sent out a mass text letting everyone know that I was back from my little unwanted vacation. Then I made my way back to Mica's arms like I'd promised her I would.

*   *   *

While I was laid up with Mica, Muffin was up chasing paper. She had just flipped the deadbolt lock on her back door behind fucking and serving a young male hustler that she had met a week ago. Muffin had barely crossed the kitchen floor when suddenly the windows beside her imploded, showering her with glass. Her immediate thought was that ol' boy's jealous girlfriend had thrown a rock through it, but as soon as Muffin's eyes landed on the dark canister lying on the floor, it blew up.

The deafening explosion knocked the wind out of her and instantly disoriented her. Scared to death, Muffin dropped to the floor and was quickly arrested by the Milwaukee Police Department's SWAT officers that poured into her place following the blast.

Chapter 20

Waking up from a much-needed nap after being up for almost twenty-four hours waiting to be released from the County jail, I was finally able to get some rest now that I was free. I sat in bed with Mica lying on me, watching me flip through the TV channels. Some ESPN sports highlights of Floyd Mayweather's career caught my attention, causing me to pause on the sports channel a bit too long for Mica's liking.

"Nooo, Bae, boxing is too violent," she blurted, expressing her dislike of what she'd assumed was my choice out of the channel surfing.

"Really?" I exclaimed, turning my attention to her. "Boxing is too violent for you when you sit here and watch *First 48* faithfully?"

"It's not the same."

"I know. One is a show about violent, senseless murders, and the other is a professional sport with athletes that's prized worldwide."

"Yeah, whateva," she retorted. "I thought you liked UFC anyways?"

"I like all of the fights. An' FYI, it's not called UFC. UFC is the company name. It's called MMA, which stands for Mixed Martial Arts. But even though MMA is more of my style, boxing is my first love. It's been around as a sport longer. I believe two of the top ten highest-paid athletes in the world are boxers. I know Floyd Mayweather has banked more money in boxing than anybody in any other sport."

My phone rang, saving Mica from more of my lecture.

"Hello?" I answered the unknown number since I had sent out the mass text letting everyone know I was back online.

"AR?"

"Who is this?" I inquired, although I recognized the female's voice. I slid out from under Mica and out of the bed.

"This Muffin. I'm in jail. I need you to come get me outta here," Muffin said in a shaky voice.

"Wait, what?" I asked as I walked out of the bedroom to talk to her. "What happened?"

"My house got raided. I don't wanna talk about it right now. AR, is you coming to get me?"

"Who you on the phone with that you had to leave the room to talk to?" Mica questioned me from the doorway of the bedroom.

"Oh, so you layin' up with yo' bitch right now?" Muffin inquired with jealousy in her voice. "Man, I didn't wanna call you, but you're all I got."

"I'm on a jail call . . . give me a second," I replied to Mica.

"Don't do that. I got you. All you gotta do is give me all the info," I said to Muffin as the one-minute warning sounded.

"This phone is about to hang up. My sister's on the phone . . . she's the one who called you. You can get everything from her."

"Okay."

"AR, you gonna come get me for real, right?" Muffin's desperation was clear.

"Yeah, I got you," I promised.

When the call ended, I felt kinda torn on what I should do. I knew that the police were watching for who came to pay the bail, and I didn't want to attach myself to whatever Muffin had done to get her crib raided. So, I asked her sister if I could bring her the four thousand dollars to go pay Muffin's bail. She agreed to take care of it as long as I gave her gas money. I ended the call and turned around to find Mica still standing there, staring at me.

"What's going on?"

"I gotta go handle something for one of my people. I don't know all of what's going on right now, but I need to run and take her sister this bail money right quick," I explained. Then I went and took a quick shower, got dressed.

"Bae, can you bring me something back to eat?"

"Text me what you want, or do you just want the money to get something for you and the boys yourself? Because I don't know how long this gon' be, and I gotta pick my daughter up from school," I explained, already knowing she was only trying to ensure that I came back to her house when I was done.

"That's fine, just go take care of yo' business. When you pick Pooh up, y'all come back here for dinner."

I agreed and walked out to my van. I went to the crib, got the money for the bail, then took it to Muffin's sister, who turned out to be a female I knew from my job as a bouncer at the club.

"Tell Muffin to call me as soon as you got her. Let her know that I gotta go get my daughter from school and I'll be there as soon as I get her settled in," I explained when I gave April the bail money.

An hour and a half later, Ms. Mica was still lying in bed, thinking of me. She felt a little suspicious about the phone call that pulled me away from her. She shifted uncomfortably, getting herself comfortable in bed and stared out the window, watching crispy clouds drifting across the skyline, shadowing out the sun. Mica really wanted to make a good impression on me, but the messiness of life just wasn't allowing her to let go of her feelings at the time.

Now, you know I've met and slept with all types of women in my young life. Some I've really liked, and some I even loved. Hell, I was coming out of a messy marriage with a woman that I thought I loved deeply. But even with all of

FO'EVA ROLLIN' 4 | ASSA RAYMOND BAKER

the years between us, D'marie's love didn't feel the way love felt with Mica. Yeah . . . yeah . . . I know every love isn't the same. I still haven't met a love like the one I had with Rhonda, but she doesn't count. And this love I feel for Mica is so different. It's something I've never felt before.

Anyways, after picking up and dropping off my daughter at Dream's place, I sat parked outside of Muffin's crib in my plum and antique gold-colored Buick Riviera, with 24-inch matching painted rims. I was lost in my thoughts, half-reading Facebook posts while I waited for Muffin's sister to drop her off to me when I decided to send Mica this text:

"My Beautiful, my heart has never opened up this complete before I met you. It's hard to explain, but being with you reminds me of all of the simple things in life. I'm sitting here thinking of our every kiss, and missing the way your body responds when I kiss you from your lips to your luscious thighs. You're all of the things I never knew I needed in a woman. To put it more simply, you feel like home."

I sent that to her and was just sitting my phone in the cup holder when it beeped and vibrated wildly, letting me know I had an incoming call.

"Yes, Luv?" I answered after seeing it was Mica calling.

"Hey, Romee, what you doing?"

"Sitting here thinking about you, obviously, from my text . . . What you doing?"

"Mr. Smartass. I'm laying here wondering why my man ain't here with me."

"Then why ain't you callin' that nigga and asking him that shit instead of fuckin' wit' me?" I joked.

"Don't fuckin' play with me, mister! You know you're that nigga I want with me."

"Do I?"

"Don't you?"

"You can't answer a question with a question."

"What do you mean? Assa, you don't think I've been showing you that all I want is you?"

"You've been showing me that all you want is me up in you," I retorted with a chuckle.

"Where's Pooh, asshole?" she inquired, laughing with me.

"I dropped her off at Dream's. They had plans already set up to go roller skating, so I let her go ahead with that." I explained just as I spotted April's car turn onto the block. "Aye, luv, I gotta go. My people just pulled up. I gotta go handle this business right quick. I'ma call you back when I'm done."

"Don't call me. Just get here as soon as you can."

"I'll be on my way as soon as I'm done," I promised, then ended the call, wondering: *should I have told her that I loved her or not?*

Chapter 21

Muffin got in the car with me so we could talk privately. When I saw her, I was kinda shocked by her appearance. She looked a mess—her hair was out of place, and she had streaks of eyeliner on her cheeks from crying while she was in police custody. I knew I shouldn't have expected her to be looking any different than what she did. It was just that I had never seen her that way, not even after we fucked.

"Damn! You look like one of those dancers from *Thriller* . . . no, no, the original *Night of the Living Dead*!" I teased, laughing while making a crucifix with my fingers. I was only trying to lighten the mood.

"Fuck you! Don't do me. I had a hard night. Catch me later and talk that shit!" she retorted, but couldn't help laughing with me. "Thank you for comin' to get me right away. A bitch really didn't wanna have to spend another night in that nasty ass jail."

"Trust me, I know the feeling . . . Now, what in the hell did you do?"

"It wasn't me. The police was on this nigga that I'd been serving weed to," she explained, dropping her head in shame. "They'd followed him to my house, and when he left, they picked him up. Then they kicked in my door looking for his shit. They found a gun on him, the weed I had just sold him, plus a baggie containing several grams of crack, they said."

"Fuck him. What did you say to 'em?" I questioned her, looking her dead in her eyes.

"I didn't tell them shit!" she answered without breaking eye contact with me. "I told 'em that I didn't know anything about what they found on him or in the house, and I don't deal drugs. I don't have anything else to say without a lawyer. Assa, I would never do anything to hurt you. You ain't been nothin' but good to me from day one. I ain't no punk bitch like that."

"Okay, Muffin, I believe you. Let's go in there and see the damage them muthafuckas done to the place. Do you got someplace to stay? 'Cause this spot is dead."

"Yeah, I already talked about that with my sister on the way over here. She said I can stay with her up in Appleton until I figure things out."

We both got out of the car and headed inside.

April had stuck around. I believe she was still there to try and help her sister in case I wanted to hurt her behind her police contact. I can fully understand why she would think that way. She didn't really know me like that. April just knows the reputation I'd made as a kick-ass bouncer at the club. I would've taken precautions if I was her too. But that thought never crossed my mind, because unlike most of the women in my life, Muffin wasn't an amateur to the game. She had been to jail and prison before, so that made her a real seasoned criminal in my book. Which is why I jam with her the long way.

When we entered Muffin's place, we were shocked that the level of destruction wasn't that bad. Normally, when the police do their drug raids, they vandalize everything. But this seemed to me to have been targeted because none of the living room furniture had been ripped open. Yeah, it had been flipped and tossed, but not really damaged. It made me wonder just how well she knew the dude that got the house raided. But now the kitchen was a different story. The police had completely vandalized it. There was broken glass everywhere I stepped, and angry footprints all on the walls and everywhere. The contents of the refrigerator had been thrown on the floor, with its doors ripped apart. Some of the cabinet doors dangled on broken hinges, with their contents tossed about, and the microwave was set on the table, torn apart.

"Fuck me! Them muthafuckas found my money. I had it hid in the back of the microwave." Muffin exclaimed, looking devastated by the loss.

"Yeah, that's fucked up. But we can get that back. Let's get yo' shit outta here and deal with the rest later," I said, a bit nonchalantly. I didn't mean to be that way. That's just how it came out.

I called my brother Ville and told him to bring my big Ford Cargo Van over. While we waited for him to arrive, the three of us gathered and packed up all of Muffin's salvageable household goods, furniture, and clothes, then put it in the front room. When Ville got there, I had him back the van up as close to the door as possible, and together, the four of us began moving all of her possessions into the back of the van and her sister's car. It took us a little over an hour to load everything into the vehicles. When we were done, I gave Muffin two hundred dollars for her pockets and told her to call me the next day. Then we went our separate ways. Ville followed them up to Appleton, and I went back over to Mica's to chill for the rest of the day.

*   *   *

Feeling that things were about to get much more serious with me, Mica felt the need to kill any and all expectations of her that might exist in the minds of the guys from her past. Her main concern was her son's father, with whom she had been having a constant affair in between and a few times behind her current no-good ex-boyfriend's back. Because of her son's father's consistency in his son's life, Mica felt it would be best to tell him that she had someone real in her life so all of the 'For Old Time's Sake' fucks they used to have would be no more.

So, she sent me a text, then got up, got dressed, and went to have the dreaded talk with him.

As I drove to her house, I imagined her waiting for me in something short, silky, and sexy. That fantasy was quickly destroyed when I received a text from her telling me that she had to make a run for her mother and handle some business of her own. Mica's text also said that she had told her cousin Lita to let me in whenever I got there. Right then, a new vision instantly took form in my mind, one that I decided to make a reality. So, I stopped at the supermarket, grabbed a few things, then headed to her house . . .

It was some time after eight-thirty p.m. when Mica pulled back up and parked in front of her house. She immediately noticed the absence of my van and any of my other vehicles that she'd become familiar with. She felt a burn of emotions that she wasn't trying to acknowledge.

"Am I crazy?" she questioned herself out loud. She couldn't be mad at me for not being at her house when she got home. It wasn't our home. She hadn't even really established herself as my girlfriend. "All we've been doing is having great sex and talking on the phone." Mica shook her head, slammed the door to her truck, and rolled her eyes in self-disgust. Walking up to her house, she tried to convince herself that what she was feeling for me was purely a physical attraction, but she knew better.

Feeling slightly downhearted, Mica pushed through the front door and stutter-stepped when her nose picked up the aroma of the late dinner I'd prepared for us. When she made it into the kitchen, she found her kids chowing down on the roast turkey, mashed potatoes, gravy, and mixed vegetables meal I'd thrown together for us. Mica's face broke into a smile when her eyes landed on me standing at the sink in a black muscle shirt, showing off my big tattooed arms, some faded black sweatpants, and socks. There were a lot of things that she'd witnessed men do for her that turned her on, but she'd never seen anything as enchanting as me standing there doing the dishes.

"What's this?" she asked, alerting us to her presence.

"Momma, this good!" her youngest son told her with his mouth full of meat and potatoes.

"Heeey, you!" I greeted her. "Let me know when you're ready to eat, 'cause I'm waiting on you. I fed them first 'cause they were acting like they were dying of starvation when I got here. They were trying to get me to buy them some McDonald's, but I cooked something instead and fooled their lil' big-head selves." I chuckled, then walked over and kissed her softly on the lips.

"Wow! I'm impressed," she said, running her hands down the length of my torso, settling on my waist. "Thank you, but you should've made them wait on me if they were acting like that."

"Leave 'em alone and go take off your coat. I'll fix our plates." I reluctantly pushed her away from me, when I really wanted to take her pretty self down right where we stood. I could see in her eyes that she was feeling the same.

Chapter 22

The love between men and women is beautiful. Mica made me feel a level of completion, of totality, that before her I'd only dreamt of having with another. I couldn't ask for more in the relationship between her and my daughter. Hell, with her and my entire family, really. Everyone who met her was accepting of her, which is a big deal because I have a lot of females in my circle who wish they was in her shoes with me. Everyone I've met in her family circle was the same with me. But with all the drama that surrounded our relationship, it made it toxic to be in.

Like things between D'marie and I . . . Just when I thought it was done and over with between us, some more bullshit kicked up behind her lying, spiteful, jealous ass. It was now months after her bullshit that landed me in jail on that trumped-up domestic violence charge, and her people were still on that with me. The big stud chick that she started fooling around with, whom everyone calls Blackie, went all out to prove to be a super gangster. Blackie identified as a man and wasn't some bum-ass nigga. Blackie had money and hands in a lot of things, from owning a nightclub to drugs and robbery.

So when Blackie got on some high-powered bullshit with me, it wasn't for play. Let's not forget that I'm pure thug and totally about that life. Drug dealing, gangbanging, pimping, and soul-snatching is just a way of life for me. That's why I had always hustled so hard to get away from it all. My goal was, and still is, to change the scenery for my children, my tribe. Muthafuckas like Blackie and D'marie, who do their best to live the stereotypes, often confuse guys like me as being weak and easy targets.

Allegedly, without D'marie's knowledge, Blackie sent a couple of goons at me to punish me for the story D'marie fed her about me beating her up because she wouldn't take me back. Now, on top of the women in my circle being dimes in looks, they are way more goal-driven, hardworking, and loyal than my ex ever was. Oh shit! I almost forgot to tell y'all that the daughter I thought I fathered with her turned out not to be mine. So yeah, that ship had sailed and sank for me. There's no going backwards for me, ever. But Blackie didn't know that.

All fam knew was that something needed to be done to me behind what D'marie had told him happened to her. So fam sent these fool-ass niggas, named Chitown and Badnews, to teach me a lesson. Blackie had them meet up with him at the bar.

"I need you to make this nigga respect my gangsta. He needs to know I ain't sweet over here. Ya feel me?" Blackie stated, taking a seat across from Chitown, who was also Blackie's cousin.

"Cuz, you know all you gotta do is point him out, and it's a done deal. All you gotta tell me is how you want this nigga served up." He drew his gun and placed it on the table. "Hospital or body bag? It's whudeva!"

"Fam, put that gun away up in my place of business! What you tryna do, run off all my customers? With yo' crazy ass." Blackie waited until he put the gun away, then told him, "I just want the nigga hurt. Not killed, just to the point that he thinks he's dead. I fuck with the nigga's baby mama and kids and shit, so you know how that is. I just need him taught a lesson. My bitch says he holdin' weight in that white and that D, so if y'all can catch him right, it can be a nice payday too."

"That's even better. A nigga in need of a good lick right now. Who is he? Do I know the nigga? Not that it matters, 'cause you're family and you know that means fuck the rest!"

"Fasho. It's the nigga AR. Do you know him?"

"Where he be at? 'Cause I know a couple of AR's. What kind of whip do he drive?" he inquired, pushing his braids out of his face and taking a drink of the complimentary beer Blackie had given him and his partners when they arrived.

"I don't know what hood he from, but I can find out from my bitch. He got all kinds of whips, but he mostly be in this gray and dark blue van or a black-on-black Tahoe on fo's."

"Oh, I think I know who you talkin' about. He be drivin' an orange and red Monte Carlo. My nigga News was just talkin' about strippin' that nigga. He be fuckin' with the bitch Muffin that sell loud. Ain't this a fuckin' coincidence."

"Some things are just meant to be," Blackie stated with a nefarious smirk. "Chi, tell folke nem to chill here and come ride with me right quick so I can show you the house I followed the niggas to the other day."

Blackie waited for Chitown to bring Badnews up to speed on things, then the two of them left the bar. Blackie drove over to my mother's house and pointed it out to them. It wasn't hard to find, because both my Tahoe and the Monte Carlo were parked on the side of the house. With his orders and target, Chitown and his two goofies got right on the mission. By the time they got on it, though, I'd been there, put up my vehicles, and gone already. I didn't live there anymore, I just stored some of my cars there in the garage. Nothing about their plan to catch me over there was ever a good idea. First of all, my mother at the time had been living at that house on 38th for like fifteen years, so everyone knows her. Second of all, Trey-eight is Ville's hood, and all he did all day and night was kick it with his guys on the block.

"Folk, I thought you said you knew where to find this punk." Badnews complained to Chitown. "I don't wanna just be sittin' out here on this hot-ass block dirty for no reason." he added, then fell back in the driver's seat.

"Fuck it, let's just run up in the crib and see what we can find?" the guy in the backseat suggested to them both.

"Fuck no. We don't know shit about that spot." Chitown immediately shot down the suggestion. "We can get from over here and just come back later, but we don't have to leave here empty-handed." He said, drawing his gun from his waistband and making sure it was ready for action.

While Chitown and his partners were staking out my mother's house, looking for me, they observed my little brother out on the block paper-chasing, serving his customers half grams of crack and weed. The three robbers were restless and thinking they had the element of surprise, so they came up with a half-cocked plan to rob Ville. I don't think they got at him because they believed he was me, since he never drove any of my whips. They didn't think Ville would bring me out to them either, because they'd never seen us together. I love my brother and enjoyed spending time with him, but the age gap between us kinda kept us apart more than I would've liked to have been. Chitown and his guys were just some thirsty-ass niggas doing clown shit.

They watched Ville stroll into the alley across from our mother's house, then Badnews put the car in drive and went in pursuit of my brother. Ville, also known as Da Villain, had spotted them long before they decided to make their move on him. As soon as he entered the alleyway, he pulled his gun and let it hang at his side, ready to put it to use. He was actually preparing to run up on them and ask 'em why they were watching the house. Ville wasn't alone; two of his guys were coming down the opposite end of the alley to meet up with him before they made their move on the guys in the unknown car. When they spotted the car turning into the alley behind Ville, that worked out better for them.

As soon as the car made it halfway to my brother, all three of 'em were on it. They started blasting at the car, making Badnews quickly throw the car in reverse in an attempt to get out of harm's way. Chitown wildly did his best to return fire out of his window, the whole time praying they made it out of there alive. Badnews whipped the car out onto the street and quickly slammed it into drive, making their getaway.

When the smoke cleared, Ville called and informed me of what happened. He was just bragging about lighting up the car, so I didn't really think nothing of it. I guessed it was some beef somebody had with them over some social media shit or something like that.

Chapter 23

Early in the A.M., just a few days after the incident with Ville, I pulled into the gas station to fill up the van after dropping my daughter off at school. Looking around, I was relieved to find the gas station not crowded with cars like it usually is when I'm forced to stop there. That morning, I needed to be in and out fast so I could get home, get changed, and get my money all tallied up before I met up with Moe to hit the highway. Our plug had called and told us he was holding his last for us, and if we didn't come get it then, we'd have to wait for the next shipment in about a week. So, yeah, I was in a rush.

When I exited the building, I noticed that two cars had pulled into the lot. One was a new-model, big-chromed-up Jaguar, with a flashy, heavy-set dude driving it. When he got out of the car, flashing a large bankroll to get the attention of a small group of high school girls waiting at the nearby bus stop, my immediate thought was, it's too early for all that. But that's new money for you. My next thought was that the second car, filled with hoodlums, was up to no good. I guessed they were going to rob the pervert.

By the time I'd gotten to pumping my gas, I received a text from Mica, just informing me that she'd made it home from work and wondering why I wasn't in her bed, ready and waiting on her. The next time I looked up from my phone, I found myself surrounded, with a gun pointed just inches from my face. I had gotten caught slippin' and there was nothing I could do about it either . . . I was caught between my van and the gas pump, with two wild-looking jack boys on each side of me.

"Fam, run that shit willingly or get dropped and make me take it off yo' body!" threatened the dreadhead with the gun in front of me. "Don't look at me, bitch-ass nigga! Get the fuck on the ground!"

"Naw, I ain't getting on the ground. Y'all can have this lil' shit I got. It ain't no need to shoot me for it," I carefully removed a big bankroll from my cargo pants leg pocket. "I won't be getting on the ground," I firmly stated, handing over the wad of small bills that totaled over $3,900.

The reason I had that much money on me in small bills that early was because I'd served my guy before I went in for the night, and since I'd spent the night away from home, I still had it with me. I was curious to know why, out of their choices between myself and the guy in the flashy car with all the jewelry on, they were robbing me instead of him. I was dressed down in my basic black work clothes. Yeah, my van was nice, but the Jag was newer and shinier. I tried but couldn't get a good look at either of their faces because they had their hats down low and their shirts pulled up, covering their noses. I watched the punk to the left of me try to open the van's door, but it was locked. My doors locked automatically when I got in and out of it. I figured his next thought would be to take the keys from me, so I dropped and kicked them beneath the van.

When he saw what I had done, he got mad and tried to hit me, but I deflected the blow, causing him to hit the top of the gas pump instead. After that, I was in full fight mode. Before I could get to it with them, I heard the flashy dude scream.

"What the fuck!" His shock at witnessing the robbery caused the jackers to run back to their maroon Buick and quickly flee the scene. I immediately dropped down, crawled under the van, and retrieved the keys. Once I had 'em, I dusted myself off and finished filling up my gas tank.

On the drive home, I recalled seeing the Buick pass me and then make a quick U-turn when I was on my way to the gas station. I didn't give it any thought because there were a lot of youngsters and old perverts out cruising the bus stops for the girls and boys, whatever, to have some fun with. From the way things went down, I knew robbery wasn't some random thing, and I wondered how long they had been following me. I went on with my plans for the day like nothing ever happened. There wasn't anything else to do but accept the loss and thank Allah that I walked away with my life, unharmed. I knew there are always two ways to handle a problem. There's a right way and a wrong way. I made the choice to hit the problem head-on and let Allah be the judge of my decision.

As I drove, I called a few of my guys and told 'em to be on the lookout for that maroon Buick Park Avenue. Lord and I went over the details of the robbery again and again as we left and returned to the state. Once back from the trip, I hit the kitchen right away so I could catch the cash waiting for me on my line. I only took a break because it was time to get my baby from school. After what happened that morning, to feel more comfortable, I swapped out of the van and got into my truck. But still, on my way to the school, I stayed looking in my rearview mirror for anything that looked out of place.

At the school, I spotted my daughter and her friend standing out front, playing around. I felt a heightened concern for her safety due to the morning's events, so I watched every car that drove by and parked in the area before I pulled up next to her. Once she got in the truck, I told her that she would have to take the bus to school for a few days because I was going to have to do some overtime at work. I dropped her off at Dream's, then headed to Moe's spot, where everyone had agreed to meet up to discuss the issue. After putting the word out on the streets, I had a few suspicious incidents take place that I thought might be related to the robbers, but I had no real proof . . .

Chapter 24

All of the mysterious robberies and attempted robberies of myself and my guys, as well as the sudden vandalism of my vehicles, had me feeling overwhelmed. Instead of taking some fun time out to spend with my girl and the kids, the sudden mysterious drama had me distracted. My mood didn't go unnoticed by Mica and others. Christmas break came, and my daughter's wish was for us to spend it together. So I shut down shop and did just that. We spent most of the break over Mica's. I don't celebrate the holiday personally, but I don't take it away from the kids. For me, it's a time to praise and reward them for being good in school and things like that. I am Muslim, so of course, I believe in Christ, just not Santa.

Anyways, Mica went out to unwind with a bunch of her family members. I was invited, but I wasn't in the big party mood that night, so I let her go alone. I chilled with the kids, watching funny movies. It was after one in the morning when I heard the alarm on my van going off. My daughter had the keys, so I kept watching *Jack Frost* and let her deal with it. A few moments after it was silenced, she came rushing into the room, telling me that someone had crashed into my van. I jumped out of bed, put on my shoes, grabbed my gun in case they wanted smoke, and rushed out of the house. When I got to the door, I was instantly furious. I saw an abandoned Dodge minivan left crashed into the side of my van.

"Go call the police over here for me," I instructed Lita, then I went to investigate the damage closer. I got in the minivan and backed it up away from mine just a little to get a better assessment. I was relieved that it was really nothing more than a deep scratch. The minivan had hit just hard enough to set off the alarm, like it had been set up to do so. I immediately scanned the area to see if it was a setup because the whole scene seemed staged to me.

I spotted the maroon Buick from the gas station robbery a few months prior, sitting idle on the next block. Before I could really decide on my next move, a black Jeep came around the corner and stopped in front of me and my daughter. It cut us off from the house so the others couldn't see what was going down from where they were on the porch. I reached around my back, gripped my gun that I'd put in my back pocket with one hand, and pushed my baby behind me with the other to shield her with my body, just in case I had to put the gun to use.

"When I say get down, I want you to get under the van right away. If you can get out on the other side and run, then do that. If you can't, then stay down. You hear me?"

"Yes," my daughter replied in a shaky voice.

"Aye, fam? Is this yo' van?" the passenger of the Jeep inquired from the window.

"Yeah, why?" I could see that there were more people in there with him, but I couldn't make out any of their faces because of the dark tint on its windows.

At that very moment, the white family that lives across the street from Mica's came outside to be nosy. Seeing them, the passenger told the driver to pull off. The Jeep did, then suddenly stopped a few feet away when they saw the elderly woman's family member getting into their car to leave.

"Aye, fam, is that yo' bitch?" the passenger of the Jeep yelled at me.

"This my daughter!" I retorted, then instantly regretted telling 'em that.

"Daddy! Here come the police," Pooh informed me loud enough for him to hear. With that, they sped off.

"Okay, go on the porch with them," I instructed her, then quickly eased my gun out of my pocket and placed it on the floor inside of my van, just in case the police wanted to get on some BS with me.

The police car went the opposite direction. They weren't the ones we called, but seeing a lot of police in the area was the norm, so I just waited beside the van for the next patrol car to come. Before that happened, both the Jeep and the Park Avenue returned. This time, they were accompanied by a Buick Riviera. I couldn't recall where I'd seen the Riviera before, but I was sure it was familiar. The Jeep stopped in front of me again, only this time, I was unarmed because I'd locked my banger in the van.

"Now what?" I questioned the passenger, getting a good look at his face this time while at the same time inching my way out in front of the van in case I had to make a run for it.

"Aye, folk, this a wannabe tough-ass nigga!" he said. I later found out he was none other than the boy Badnews. His comment tickled the others in the Jeep with him. Then he pulled his gun, and the back door of the Jeep opened. But before his partner could get out, or anything else could go down, the old lady saved my ass again by coming outside to be nosy some more.

"Hey there! I called the cops for you. They should be here in a few," she informed me as she walked toward me, holding a steaming coffee mug.

"Okay, thank you!" I was grinning when I turned back to the guys in the Jeep. "She said the police should be on their way here, so y'all might wanna just go on and leave," I repeated, staring Badnews down while keeping my sight on the weapon he was holding just below the window. They pulled off again, and so did the other cars. This let me know that they were all in cahoots with the shit.

"Your friends should not be speeding through here like that," the lady said in disgust.

"I agree. They're not my friends, though. I didn't know them. I think they might have something to do with this accident. I don't know what's going on for sure, but you should go in the house because they have guns. I believe they're on something shady."

"Oh my! I'm going to call the police again. You be careful out here now," she told me before going back in her house.

I ordered the kids and everybody to go in the house as well. I gave them strict instructions not to come back outside for anything. I planned on hiding in the van and waiting to see if they came back to try to do a home invasion or whatever they had on their minds. If they did come back, I was going to jump out, blasting on them. I had my gun ready for them when Mica called me, telling me that she was about to pull up to the house. I did my best to let her know what was going on without saying too much on the phone.

A few minutes later, she was turning the corner, and so was the Jeep. I didn't see the other cars this time. Badnews didn't say anything else to me; he just stared at me as one of his guys, who I found out was the punk Chitown, got out of the Jeep and into the minivan. Then they both took off. As soon as they drove away, their buddies in the Park Avenue and the Riviera came driving by, waving their guns in the air in childish intimidation tactics. Needless to say, that shit didn't work. They were lucky Mica was standing by my side, or I would've emptied my clip through their car windows. Since they thought they wanted to get on some real gangsta shit with the thug.

The police finally came, pulling up a minute or so later, missing them all by seconds. I shook my head, but that's how they treat us in the hood. With the help of the nosy neighbor, I explained to them what went down as far as the accident went. The police made the report and then left. Approximately ten minutes later, they called me, notifying me that the minivan had been stolen from just a few blocks away from Mica's house. With that bit of information, I didn't get much sleep that night. Early the following afternoon, I called up some of the Brothas that I knew were close by and had them ride down on me. I put them up on both of the vehicles and let them know what I thought was going on with the situation. Since the jack boys now knew where my girl lived, I had my guys keep security on her place. I also made it my business to be there as much as I could to make sure she was good, personally. If they were smart, they wouldn't be too quick to run up in Mica's place knowing that now their hand had been exposed.

Chapter 25

Just a few months back, life was as normal as it could be for me. I was getting the hang of what it truly means to be an active father, so my children and I were good. I had money flowing in like a river. I'd gotten closer with Mica. My family was better than they'd been in a long time. Things in the ghetto were good. Then all of the bullshit with D'marie and Blackie happened. Now I was overwhelmed. I decided to use the turn of the year to spread the word that I was done with the games. I was making my last run. It touched me when I informed Mica of my decision and she didn't cut and run away.

"I know, Bae, that you're not used to having someone helpin' you. I see that."

"I gotta take responsibility for the messes I cause directly or indirectly." Being the man I am, I try not to mix my street life with my home life. Just like I don't bring bullshit from my past relationships into my next one.

"Yeah, but a'ight, you can't control everything on your own."

"Nobody can solve my problems the way I can."

"You're not alone anymore. You have a woman to help you . . ."

"You can encourage me and support me in a crisis, but ultimately, in the end, only I can take the proper steps to correct my problems."

"You're only human, Bae. It doesn't mean that you're weak if you accept help when you need it. Sometimes you have to let people help you. Especially the one who loves you. Let me help!"

Mica recognized that my hesitance had more to do with me being cautious than anything else. She was right though. The last few days had been exhausting on me, both physically and mentally. I really wasn't sure if she was the one I was supposed to be with back then, but she really believed in me and was willing to go through the fire with me. I felt like she deserved more of me. I didn't have a ring to place on her finger, so I removed a few links and gave her my silver, black onyx, and diamond bracelet as a placeholder for my promise of love.

Two days later, I took her with me to Appleton to meet up with Muffin to deliver her order and pick up the cash she had for me. To be sure I didn't miss her, Muffin left an extra keycard at the front desk for me. When we got up to Appleton, I didn't want to be riding around with the drugs on me, so I went to the hotel to drop it off in the room before we did any sightseeing. Believing that we had some time before Muffin made it there, I asked Mica to come up to the room with me.

In the elevator on the way up, I worked on getting me a little quickie in with Mica, and she was with it. Just not on the busy elevator. I just knew Muffin wasn't gonna be there yet, but she was. I heard her talking on the phone as soon as we entered the room. I was like, damn. When I saw her sitting there, I didn't tell her I was bringing anyone with me. Mica instantly caught a little attitude and turned to leave. I quickly stopped her, took her by the arm, and spun her around until she was facing Muffin. I held Mica firmly in my arms.

"Whoa, I don't think you really want to do that," I said, speaking softly in her ear and holding her close to me. I saw that Muffin wasn't trippin' about her being there, so I went for it. "I think this is meant to go like this. We came up here to have some fun, so let's all have fun." I loosened my grip on Mica's arm, then as nonchalantly as I could, made introductions. Neither one of them said a word. I was still confident that I knew the type of women I was dealing with. They both craved the dominance of a true thug like myself.

"What are you talkin' about?" Mica inquired with a hint of something in her voice that wasn't anger. She didn't even try to free herself from my hold.

"I think y'all need to be pleased and to please me," I answered her, then glanced at Muffin and said, "And Muffin, you're gonna do whatever the fuck I ask you to do." Muffin looked puzzled for a moment, then smiled, still not saying a word. "Tell her that you want her to stay."

"Stay and play," Muffin said without question, just widening her smile.

"Play?" Mica exclaimed, now with a telltale smirk on her lips as she stared at me through the mirror on the wall behind where Muffin sat waiting for us.

"Muffin, stand up and show us what you're working with."

Muffin's freaky ass stood up from the bed and slowly turned around, showing off her body. She wore a short, hot pink satin and lace one-piece short pants outfit that was unbuttoned down the front, showing off all of her cleavage, right down to her little butterfly rainbow belly ring. On her feet were a pair of matching pink tennis shoes with four-inch wedge heels.

"If you like what you're seein', then don't just stand there, come and play," she invited us, running her long tongue across her glossy lips.

"Hmmm, nice," I approved, releasing Mica's waist. "So, what you finna do?" I questioned her, stepping around her and walking over to the bed. I tapped Muffin on the butt, then sat down and stretched my legs out on the bed.

"I'ma stay," Mica shyly replied.

"Good, now take off your shirt," I ordered her, keeping my voice low but firm. I retrieved my phone and started recording. Mica's hands slightly shook with excitement as she pulled her white baby doll top off over her head. She tossed it on the chair beside her. "Now the bra." Mica took an audible breath. Before she could protest, I told her to take it off again. She released a big long sigh as she complied with my demands.

Without saying a word to her, Muffin stripped down to her birthday suit, keeping on the heels so that she kinda towered over Mica. I guess it was a way of showing dominance between her and Mica. I don't know. The whole scene was just so sexy to me. I could see Muffin's eyes locked on the bulge of my erection locked away in my jeans as she waited for me to give further instructions.

"Both of y'all come here and give me a kiss. Then I wanna see y'all kiss each other," I commanded, and they obeyed, giving me a juicy double kiss that quickly turned into a hot girl-on-girl make-out party.

They plopped down beside me on the bed. I gave them some room and focused on recording the best I could. I was getting more and more aroused by the sight taking place in front of me between my girl and my friend. Seeing that they were busy getting to know each other, I used the time to take my shirt and pants off in preparation to join in.

"Mica?" I called her attention to my hardness pressing against my boxer briefs, eager to be freed.

"Ummmm, yes, Daddy," she purred, pulling away from Muffin, who continued kissing and sucking on her neck.

"Rub her box."

"I can't . . . I never . . ."

"I didn't ask you what you ever did. I said rub her box."

"Here, let me show you how I like it," Muffin spoke up, then immediately twisted her long braids into a loose knot in the back of her head to keep it from obstructing my view.

"I wanna see her cum in her panties," I informed Muffin since she took over.

The little dominatrix replied by instantly hiking Mica's skirt up around her waist and pushing her down on the bed. Then she cupped her breasts and pinched her nipples before commencing to suck on Mica's breasts while simultaneously brushing her fingertips over the center of the sexy fabric. I saw Mica shiver and swallow, then moan with pleasure as Muffin's fingers swirled over her mound.

I couldn't take just watching anymore, so I scampered over to Mica and presented my throbbing knight to her. She smiled at it, wet her lips, then sucked my tip between her soft lips. While she sucked me, Muffin made her way down Mica's body. We locked eyes, then she used her teeth to pull the moist panties out of her way. I watched her swirl and saw her fingers in her all the while, never breaking eye contact with me.

"Make her cum for me," I said right as Mica took me in her throat. "Use your tongue on her."

Following my orders, Muffin purred with lust as she found Mica's love button, then buried her face in her creaming center. My head swiveled between the action as I watched them both perform orally. I can't lie, it did take long before seeing Muffin work on Mica and feeling Mica's warm mouth on me made me erupt buried in her throat. Surprisingly, she milked my hardness for every drop that she'd been working for.

Chapter 26

While I was recuperating, I received a call from one of my guys who was in the next town over, asking if I could come meet him halfway there with his usual order. I had half of what he wanted with me right then, so I told him he could meet me at the hotel.

Spent from my release, I fell back against the headboard and enjoyed the show the girls were putting on below me. Before long, Muffin had Mica bucking against her mouth as she soaked her chin.

"Ahh, yesss, it's my turn," Muffin exclaimed, sliding up from between Mica's knees. Not bothering to wipe the cum from her face, Muffin took my semi-erect length in her cum-soaked hand, and with the other, Mica allowed her to guide her mouth right where Muffin needed it to be. All of that bullshit Mica tried talking earlier about never being with another woman before was just that—bullshit. Without the slightest bit of hesitation, Mica cupped Muffin's plump ass and pulled her against her mouth. Mica plunged her skillful tongue as deep as she could inside of her, then commenced to licking and sucking on her with a skill that I didn't know she had.

Panting from the pleasure that Mica was giving her, Muffin attempted to stroke and suck me back hard again. It wasn't her mouth work that got me up again; it was the erotic sounds coming from the two of them that got me there. I took Muffin by the ponytail and fucked her mouth for a moment before I rolled away, pulling my hardness from her lips. I got off the bed, grasped Mica by the legs, and pulled her until her hips were at the edge of the bed, then dove balls deep between her thighs.

My thrusts were long, hard, and sure. Now it was Muffin cumming. She threw her head back, screaming and rolling her hips while still straddling Mica's face. I pulled her down flat on top of Mica and switched. I could still feel Muffin's box twitching as she came again. This time with me pounding her out right on top of Mica, with her sucking on her breasts. Muffin tapped out, leaving Mica all to me. I immediately dropped down for a taste. Then I climbed on the bed and flipped her over on all fours and went to pounding her from behind. Face down, with me gripping her hips, Mica took it all.

Muffin took over recording. She maneuvered the phone just right so we could all watch our show together later. Sweat-drenched, I pounded her harder and harder, just the way I knew she liked it. I was starting to think that I'd bitten off more than I could handle by suggesting the threesome, but soon I felt the hint of her center begin clenching my length just before she started cumming. She felt so good, I busted again and again right along with her before I collapsed on top of her.

The homie Nut texted, telling me he would be pulling up to the hotel in five minutes or so, so I quickly got myself together, then went down to meet up with him. Outside, light snow flurries were falling, but it wasn't cold out. Had it been cold, Nut would have been ass out after me waiting ten minutes for him to pull up. He came fifteen minutes later than he said he would. We made our exchange, then went our separate ways. On my way back inside the hotel, I heard a no-nonsense male voice from behind me.

"Stop right where you are! Keep your hands where I can see them!"

Turning slowly around, I saw two police officers standing there, but with their guns drawn, pointing at me. I dropped my head and did as they ordered me to.

"What's this about?"

"We just have a few questions for you. If you're not our guy, then you're free to go on your way. Is that fair enough?" One of the officers explained while his partner removed everything from my pockets, making sure to take the money I had just collected from Nut.

Knowing that I didn't have anything incriminating on me but that cash, I agreed. I was still handcuffed and walked back to their car. A short time later, an unmarked detective car pulled up with super dark tinted windows. I just knew it was over for me right then. Everything about the car screamed it was the feds. I couldn't even tell the girls what was going on because I couldn't risk the police going up to the room and finding the rest of the work that was in the room. Since I'd only planned on running out to meet Nut and come right back, I didn't have my phone with me to alert the girls before I was hauled off to jail. One of the officers walked over to the car and spoke in a hushed voice to someone through the slightly opened window, then he returned with a disappointed expression on his face.

"He's not our man. Cut him loose," he informed his partner, who went to hesitantly uncuffing me.

"Why do you have so much money on you?" he questioned, looking for a reason to take me to jail.

"I buy, sell, and trade cars for a living. I just sold a 1973 Oldsmobile Cutlass in great condition literally minutes before you guys stopped me."

That wasn't totally untrue. I did sell Nut that car that he was in, just not that day. I used it in my answer because I knew they had seen me talking to him in it before they stopped me. The whole situation made me think they were watching him.

"How long do you plan on being in Appleton?"

"I plan on getting out of here in a couple of hours or so. My girlfriend wants to visit the mall before we go. You know how shit goes, we make the money, and they spend it," I joked, trying to lighten the mood.

"Thank you for your cooperation. Have a good rest of your stay," the officer said, letting me go free.

I praised Allah all the way back up to the room. When I stepped off of the elevator, I damn near ran into Muffin standing there with Mica peeking out into the hallway from the room. They were looking for me. I told them what happened, and we all agreed that it was checkout time.

Chapter 27

Five, four, three, two, one. Happy New Year!

I brought in that new year with Mica and the kids. I'd made it through to another one. No, things weren't as good as I would've liked them to be, but I had all of the real things in my life that hold true value to me: Mica and the kids.

Mica had some running around to do that morning, so I decided to use the free time to go check on my mother's house since she was out of town with her boyfriend. Riding around with my daughter, I drove while she sat beside me on her phone, kickin' it with her friends on Facebook, while at the same time controlling the music. I'll tell you, that girl loved her some Pretty Ricky. I shook my head every time she pressed play.

I came to a stop on Thirty-Fifth and North Avenue. When I glanced to the right, I spotted the black Jeep and Buick Riviera, with their occupants—Blackie, Chitown, Badnews, and two unknowns—standing right beside them, talking. Right then and there, I found out that everything I'd been going through was at the hand of D'marie's people. As soon as the light permitted, I sped the fuck off before I lost my reasonable thinking and let my three-five-seven disturb the peace. If my baby wasn't with me at the time, I would've made a mess. I was so mad that I skipped checking on my mom's crib. I needed to put as much distance between them and myself as fast as I could. When my van came to rest, we were at my cousin Chocolate's crib way out in the hundreds.

My daughter and I went inside. I gave Chocolate the whole story of everything that's been going on with me because of my ex-wife's bullshit. It felt good to talk, and I really needed her to be a voice of reason.

"Cuz, I know that bitch ain't that stupid. I mean, how many years were y'all married? I think you should try talking to D'marie or better yet, her sister. Because all the bitch gonna do is lie to save her bitch. You still talk to her sister, don't you?" Chocolate asked while rolling herself another blunt.

"Yeah, I talk to her, but she ain't finna do shit but lie for her ass too. The only one who will probably tell me the truth is her lil' brother. I'll holla at him."

By the time I left my cousin's house, I'd made up my mind to have that conversation with my brother-in-law. I went right to Dream's house and dropped my daughter off to her for the night. After I did that, I called my ex-wife's punk ass to ask her about the shit myself, but she didn't answer. I couldn't ride down on her to talk to her face to face because she had moved out of the house that we shared when we were together, and I had no clue where she'd moved to. I ended up talking to D'marie's sister, La'tisha. She confirmed that Blackie was known for setting people up to be robbed, as well as told me that Blackie felt some type of way about what D'marie had told her that I'd done to her. La'tisha claimed not to know where her sister had moved to either. I really didn't care where she moved to; I just wanted to know where my enemies lay their heads. I mean, fair is fair, right?

One of my plans for the new year was to finalize my divorce and ask Mica to move away with me and my daughter. I knew I would need to get a real nice amount of money up real quick before I did that. Because I would've been asking Mica to leave her job, uproot her kids, and all of that to start over with me. I know I said I was done with the game, but for this, I called up my old plug and told him I needed to touchdown. If it wasn't for finding out who exactly was behind all of the nonsense that was going on with me, I promise you I would've made that call.

"Moe, will you be ready in the morning?" I asked, counting out and banding up stacks of cash on the bed.

"I'm ready for you now. I'm on my way up there by you tonight to fuck wit' my lil' bitch. She been cryin' 'bout a nigga ain't been spending enough time with her and shit. You know how emotional they get when they knocked up." He chuckled. "I'ma hit you when I touch and just kill two birds with one trip."

"I'm pretty sure that's not how the saying goes, but I got you." I teased and laughed. "I only got a quarter or two for you, bro bro."

"You good, bro. That's right on time. I gotta give my bitch like ten for the bills and baby stuff."

I actually felt better than I had in months after that call. I had something else to focus on instead of stressing over the D'marie and Blackie drama. Feeling restless, I decided to work out. While I was at it, I posted a few selfies on Facebook, jokingly asking my female followers if anyone wanted to come wash my back for me in the shower. Like, as soon as I posted that, I got a call from Mica talkin' shit about my pics and post.

"Bae, you know I ain't serious. I'm just fuckin' around. You're all I want and need to take care of me."

"Umm, I hear your lips movin'," she said. "Stop showing my shit to them thirsty-ass hoes! Don't make me be late for work!" She threatened me.

I assured her that I was joking, then asked her to call me when she got settled in at work. Ending the call, I went and took that shower that got me cussed out. Alone! Afterwards, I used my free time to work on the novel I'd been writing titled *Vengeful Guidance*. Publishing some of my stories was another one of my goals that I'd set for myself that year. D'marie never supported my dream of becoming a serious writer, so I put it on the back burner when we were together. Hell, she put so much on my plate, I didn't have time for it.

With a new start and someone real in my world, I was back on it. In hindsight, that damn D'marie didn't do shit but hold me back and cause me more pain than anything. I promise you, I miss her . . . NOT!

I was just minding my business when . . .

Ms. Pretty you came walking in / My heart stopped to say what is this / Just soon as you started talking / Something happened deep within me / All of a sudden I got this feeling when a...

I was laying across my bed writing and listening to R. Kelly's song *"You Made Me Love You"*, when the ringing of my phone snapped me out of a steamy love scene. It was Moe texting me that he'd made it up to the Mil. Seeing the time was almost two in the morning, my first mind was to tell him that I would hit him in a few hours, but I kinda felt like if I didn't go get it from him now, I would miss out. So I responded, telling him that I'll meet him in the hood on Twenty-Fourth and Capital. Then I got dressed, gathered my cash and things, then headed out.

Chill came from feet to head / And then I / Turned away from you and / Said to myself. This is not supposed to happen / Brother, you've been hurt too many times before / First I slipped, then I tripped, then fell... You made me love you, bae / Made me love you, bae / Made me love you, bae...

I hummed the words to the song in my van on my way to the garage to swap out for my Riviera. I don't know why I didn't drive the Tahoe since a light snow was falling. For some reason, the car just felt right at the time.

I got the car and stopped at the gas station on Twenty-Seventh and Capital to get me something to drink and to kill some time since Moe hadn't arrived yet. I had just gotten back in the car when he called, asking me where I'm at, like he's been waiting long.

"Man, I been there! I'm on my way back. I'm around the corner." I told him, dumping the money out of the cloth Royal Crown sack into the black plastic bag I'd gotten with my purchase. For some reason, I've always liked those sacks, and that was my last one. Believe it or not, they're hard to come by when you're not a drinker. Anyways, I was pulling away from the pump when I spotted Blackie turning onto the lot. I was instantly heated, but I knew it wasn't the right time. Reluctantly, I kept it moving.

Chapter 28

When you have two hearts working towards the same goal, you tend to make similar moves. Like, while I was out tryna get money up so I could truly live life with Mica, she was out making sure that nothing got in the way of that from her past.

Mica entered the South Side nightclub dressed in her work uniform. The cozy nightclub's dim lighting, dark-colored walls, and smooth jazzy music put her in the mind of an old-time juke joint. No, it wasn't her type of place, but it was cool to have a friendly meet-up in. She scanned the room, looking for her persistent ex-boyfriend. Mica had agreed to meet up with him because she was sick of his constant calls and texts all hours of the day and night, begging her to allow him to apologize and hoping to get another chance to be with her. No, she hadn't forgiven or forgotten what he'd done to her. The only reason she agreed to the face-to-face meeting was because he had picked a public place that wasn't too far from her job. Mica planned to hear him out, then make him understand that she's happily involved with me.

Not spotting him at any of the tables in the dim corners of the place, Mica took a seat at the bar. She glanced at the time on her phone, seeing that she still had over an hour before she had to be at work. That's also when she saw the Facebook posts I made. She had just hung up with me when the bartender stepped in front of her, ready to take her order. Feeling slightly jealous and a bit guilty, she briefly considered ordering a double shot of Patron, but ordered a 7-Up over ice instead. The bartender quickly placed her drink on the counter.

"I got it," BG said, appearing beside Mica out of thin air. He slapped a twenty-dollar bill down in front of her and the bartender. "Can I also have a couple of shots of Patron to go with this?" he ordered, then turned to Mica. "My bad for making you wait. I had to handle a lil' business on the way here," he explained, making sure she saw his bankroll before he put it in his pocket.

"It's okay. I just got here myself. Now that we're here, wassup? You know I gotta be at work in a lil' while, so say what you gotta say."

"Damn, you know you look good!" he complimented as he took a seat beside her. This was the same thing he'd said to himself when he saw her walk through the door of the club from his hiding place in the back beside the jukebox. "I really been missin' you."

"I'm not doing this with you, BG. If you don't got shit else to say, I'm leaving!" Mica said, her face suddenly twisting in annoyance.

"Mica, don't be like that. I'm not tryna make you madder than I know you've been with me. I'm just . . . just kinda nervous," he admitted, reaching around her toward the drinks. "Here, have a shot with me. I know you gotta go to work, but we both know that one shot ain't gonna do shit but help you relax a little," he pressed, handing her the tainted drink.

"BG, I'm going to hear you out, but I need you to know that I'm in a relationship. I'm happy where I am in life right now. I need you to understand and respectfully stop calling me at all hours of the day," she told him, then drank the shot, chasing it with the soda.

*   *   *

Parked on Twenty-Fifth Street just off the corner sat Moe's rose gold Infiniti. I made a swift U-turn and parked right behind it. Before anything, I slipped my gun in my coat pocket, grabbed the cash bag, and then got in with him.

"I know one thing, you better not ever say shit 'bout me being more low-key when you out here makin' moves in this," I complained, while checking out the interior of the truck. I spotted Blackie's car creeping down the block.

"Let's not forget, bro, I wasn't comin' up here for this. This move's especially for you, remember?"

"Sure, blame it on the needy!"

"Get the fuck outta here wit' that needy shit!" he chuckled, then told me that he left the work at his girl's crib because he saw too much police action on his way to her place for him to keep riding around with it in the flashy vehicle.

I handed him the money bag and told him that I'd meet him in the Wendy's parking lot instead of on the street. We parted ways. I knew already that he would take his sweet time meeting me, especially since he said his girlfriend was already trippin' about him not spending much time with her. So, I went cruising the strip, sightseeing more or less. There's always something going on in that hood, no matter what time of day or night it is.

On my way back down Capital, heading towards Wendy's on Twenty-Seventh Street, I passed the Jeep heading in the opposite direction. I paid the fools no mind, keeping my focus on what I was out there to do. I stopped at the gas station across the street from my destination to kill time. While I was there, I picked up some snacks. When I walked out to my car, I observed Blackie sitting there. He had followed me back and was sitting in the car, talking on the phone and watching me.

Now, I couldn't ignore it. I never really believe in coincidences, so seeing the punk there put me more on alert. My thoughts were that Blackie was on the phone with the flunky bunch in the Jeep, preparing to get on some BS that I didn't have time for.

I shook my head, trying more so to shake away the cruel thoughts that were trying to take up residence in my mind. I got in my car and pulled right off. I headed away from where I was supposed to be going. Instead of leading them to my plug, I quickly sped down Capital Drive.

You guessed right if your guess is I ran into the punk in the Jeep. Not liking the direction the predicament was looking to go, I thought it would be best to call my plug and tell him to hold off until I called him. In my irritation, I dropped my phone. To make it worse, it fell down between the seats, causing me to take my eyes off the rearview mirror. That's when the Jeep rammed my car from behind so hard that if I wasn't wearing my seatbelt, I might've gone headfirst through the windshield.

"What the fuck, man!" I snapped, looking over my shoulder at the fools. I'd barely gotten back focused on the road when I was rammed again. This time, I had to suddenly cut the steering wheel hard to the left to stop from crashing into a row of parked cars. It's a good thing I keep my vehicles in top-notch running condition, or it would've been over for me. But the Riviera responded the way it needed to, preventing the catastrophe.

Chapter 29

Gradually becoming more unhinged, the lovesick BG sat with his arms folded across his chest, watching Mica. At the same time, he kept an eye on the time on his phone, figuring the drug he had slipped in her soda should take effect in about ten minutes or less. In his deranged state of mind, he thought about dosing her again, but only smiled and continued to sip on his beer instead.

Riding a woozy wave, Mica's ex was able to convince her to move from her seat at the bar to one of the tables. He led her to a table beside the replica vintage jukebox and the exit. When they got there, the rock song "Behind Those Eyes" by *Three Doors Down* began, and Mica, for some reason, zeroed in on the words.

You said I got something to day / Then you got that look in your eye / There is something you got to know / And you said it as you started to cry / I've been down this road before / And I swear I'll never go there again / I've seen this face once before / And I don't think I can do it again / I've seen this face before / And I don't think I can do it again / There's something I can't see / There's something different in the way you smile . . .

Mica saw BG talking to her but her attention kept returning to the song. She tried her best to concentrate but the words kept fading in and out. The song droned on and on. Eventually, she couldn't understand it anymore. She had to close her eyes, when she could no longer fight the pull of the drug another moment.

As you turn and walk away / I saw another look in your eye / Even though it hurt like it did / No, no / You say now that it hurt you the same / Is there something here to believe / Or is it just another part of the game / There's something different in the way you smile / Behind those eyes you lie / Because I'm never going to change your mind / Behind those eyes you hide...

Mica's eyelids fluttered a bit and finally closed. She was out.

When Mica began to fall out of the chair, BG caught her. Then, as nonchalantly as he could be, he leaned her against him and pulled her towards the exit. When the cold night air hit Mica's face, she became aware that she was no longer inside.

"What's going on?" she slurred, slightly opening her eyes. "I'm cold."

"It's okay, go back to sleep," he replied as he helped her walk through the light street traffic of Forest Home Avenue.

One of the last things Mica noticed before passing all the way out again was being dropped in a seat and a car door slamming shut.

*   *   *

I stomped on the gas, accelerating to law-breaking speeds, jetting away from them fools on the straightaway. With a nice distance between us, I quickly bent a few corners, then slipped into the alley. I stopped and shut off my lights to hide my position. I pulled my gun from the pocket of my tan and bronze-colored Gucci hoodie, then waited. Staring across the yard between the sleeping houses, I saw the Jeep shoot past on the block over. I gave it a few minutes, then drove out of the alley. I made a right turn instead of a left, just in case they had made a U-turn looking for me.

I should have gone with my first mind and turned left because I met right up with them at the corner. We both just sat there a moment, staring at one another. I wished the punks would just go on and let me be, but I knew that wasn't finna happen. I said, "Fuck it," and drove across the intersection, never taking my eyes off of them. Suddenly, the Jeep launched forward.

"Stupid muthafuckas!" I yelled, when the fools tried to ram me in the midst of me crossing the four-way intersection. Thinking fast, I cut the wheel hard to the right, just avoiding the collision.

In the dim lighting, I could just make out the driver laughing at me. The passenger leaned out the window, pointing a gun at me as a challenge or for intimidation, or maybe both. At this point, I'd had enough of their bullshit. The niggas really thought they had me shook. My mind instantly slipped into the red zone. I threw my car in reverse, straightened it up, then pushed it back into drive while lowering my window and snatching my gun from my lap. I started blowing at them right there in the middle of the street.

At the time, shooting at 'em seemed like a bright idea, but I quickly emptied my clip into the front of the hasty reversing Jeep. But when I emptied, it was their turn, and their gun held a clip as long as my forearm. When he squeezed the trigger, his Glock spit like a machine gun. I was already putting my car's turbocharged engine to use by that time, though. They got right on my ass, chasing me as I zigzagged through the dark streets. I was glad it was so late because traffic was light, which made it easier to maneuver as fast as I was going.

When I turned onto Thirty-first Street, my back tire blew out. I don't know if it happened from the shots at me or just disintegration from my wild driving. I heaved the steering wheel to the right and quickly back to the left. As it spun across the snow-slick road and onto the sidewalk on the other side of the street, I yanked the steering wheel back the other way. But the car's balance was gone, and its brakes were useless. The car clipped the metal post of the guardrail. I knew the car couldn't hold up, so I braced myself against the seat and squeezed my eyes shut as the car flipped and rolled. When the roof caved in and I felt shattered glass cascade over me, my mind went to my kids. The car flipped one last time, landing upside down. I thought I was done for.

I found my breath and immediately went to work on getting out of the wreckage. I crawled out into the cold water of the shallow creek. I looked frantically for the Jeep in the confusion. I heard footsteps approaching and took off running down the dark creek bed. Running my ass off, I made it to my mother's crib, so I just got in the van and went home. That's when I realized that I had hurt my leg in the accident. I parked on the side of my house and scanned my surroundings, looking for any sign of more trouble before I got out.

In killer pain now, I half-limped inside the house, went straight into my bedroom, and right away got out of the filthy, freezing wet clothes and into a hot shower. Knowing if I didn't get in there right away, I would be sick with the flu.

Chapter 30

Whatever the nigga gave her had my love knocked out cold for like two hours. When Mica woke up, she was confused and disoriented in the gloomy, unfamiliar room. She vaguely remembered being carried someplace by someone whose face she couldn't remember clearly. She felt a dull pain on her left side and knew her bruised ribs were from being held around her waist too tightly. At the time, she was too woozy and confused to focus on anything. All she wanted to do was sleep, but she knew something about her situation wasn't right.

Instead of letting her eyes close again, Mica sat up. She moved a little too fast, kicking off a pounding headache that caused a wave of nausea. She felt like she was going to be sick. Out of the corner of her eye, she saw the open door to the bathroom. Weakly, she pushed herself to her feet. Quickly, she staggered to the toilet and threw up. When she was done emptying her guts, she leaned on the dirty toilet seat for a few moments before attempting to stand again. Mica carefully stood up, using the sink for balance.

Not feeling much better, she glanced in the mirror over the sink. When she saw her sickly reflection, she turned on the cold water, splashed some on her face, then rinsed her mouth out before taking a drink from the tap. The feeling of the cold water on her skin cleared some of the haziness. When she was a bit more alert, Mica ambled back into the other room where she saw nothing but a faded blue futon that she'd obviously slept on and her purse on the trash-littered floor. She scanned the room, feeling the panic building within her.

Mica had no clue where she was. She stepped further into the room, and that's when she noticed the stale odor and saw that the windows were all boarded up. That's when she really started to panic. She rushed to the door on the opposite side of the room, snatched it open, only to find her crazy ex-boyfriend standing there holding a blanket and looking just as surprised as she was to see him standing there. A sudden, violent wave of dizziness hit her, making her knees buckle.

BG dropped everything, rushed in, and caught her before she hit the floor. Holding her unconscious body close to his, he dragged her back over to the futon, laying her down and stealing a kiss from her lips.

* * *

Moving on autopilot, I went through all of the proper precautions that one must go through after something like that. I called and reported the car accident. That's when I found out that I'd lost the phone I needed to get in touch with my plug. I needed that phone so I could get the work he had for me, or the money back so I could get better prepared for what could come my way after all that BS with them assholes in the Jeep.

Honestly, I still wasn't thinking clearly, so I redressed, replaced the gun I lost with another, then headed back over to the crash scene. The police were there, having the mangled Riviera pulled out of the creek when I got there. Seeing the damaged car made everything flash through my mind, from the car chase, to the shooting, to every damn thing. I thanked the Lord for allowing me to continue on with my life. There was no other way possible that I could have lived through the crash with no real harm done to me without there being some holy intervention.

Chapter 31

The next time Mica awoke, her mind was clearer. She couldn't believe her crazy ex had kidnapped her. Angry, she felt her panic building again. Using it as motivation, Mica sprang to her feet and rushed to the door. She frantically tried the door knob. That's when she heard a low growl coming from behind her. She whipped herself around and found a vicious-looking Pitbull with its intense eyes trained on her. The dog's ears were back, its lips curled, showing its deadly teeth.

Instantly, a memory of one of BG's mutts ripping the throat out of another dog during a dog fight that he'd forced her to attend with him popped into her mind. It was enough to make her pause on her escape attempt. Mica stood very still, almost not breathing, as she stood in the middle of the room. Not seeing a way out of the situation, her panic got stronger. Right when she was about to do something stupid, she heard the toilet flush. Seconds later, her captor walked out of the bathroom and found her frozen with fear in front of the dog.

"Chill!" he commanded the mutt. The dog obediently relaxed, planting itself on the floor but clearly still on guard duty.

"I see you finally woke up. Where were you going? Come over here and sit with me." BG gestured toward the futon where he sat down.

"BG, what in the hell do you think this is?" Mica shouted. "What? You put something in my drink? You fuckin' drugged me!" At the sound of her hot aggression, the dog rose to its feet with its gaze fixed on her. It gave a warning with a frightening, snarling growl that made Mica check her tone. "Get that thing, BG, before it bites me."

"She ain't gonna do shit I don't tell her to do. I'll take her away if you chill and play nice." He gestured toward the seat beside him again.

"Whatever. Just get this damn dog outta here." She agreed, but didn't move until he locked the mutt in the bathroom.

Watching the punk secure the dog, Mica's mouth threatened to fill with bile at the thought of being close to BG. But seeing no other choice, she hesitantly joined him on the futon, choosing a seat on the opposite end, facing him. As soon as her ass touched the futon, he scooted next to her and began rubbing her thigh, causing every muscle in her body to become rigid.

"Relax, girl. Damn . . . I know I did some fucked-up shit to you in the past . . . babe, it's . . . it's how you make me get because I love you so much. I'm not gonna . . ."

"BG, you don't love me."

"I do love you, Mica! Don't fuckin' tell me how the fuck I feel!" he snapped, raising his hand like he was going to hit her. Mica quickly pushed him away and jumped to her feet.

"I'm sorry, Mica! Babe, I'm sorry, please sit down. I'm not gonna hit you. I'm just trippin' 'cause I've been sipping. Babe, you know how that sauce sometimes gets me. You got my head all fucked up acting the way you're acting. Come sit down and let me show you I love you."

She couldn't believe that she ever had felt anything for the crazy muthafucka. She couldn't believe the bullshit he was saying. Mica began to tremble but then glanced at the door. She pushed it all away and came up with a plan after remembering how he always fell asleep immediately after they fucked. Glancing at the door again, she decided to give him what he really wanted.

"I love you too."

"Yeah, right, bitch. You love me, but you got that bitch-ass nigga all living with you. Playin' house and shit!"

"No, no, he don't live with me," she retorted, wondering how long he had been watching the house. "I do love you. I just hate when you drink too much because you get like this. BG, I miss you." She lied, sitting back down beside him. "I hate how your drinking makes you act. You say you miss me. If that's true, don't fight me. Show me I'm really what you want," she said seductively as she could.

Just as she hoped it would, BG's lust overpowered his better judgment. He scooted closer. When he leaned over her to kiss her, she could smell the onions and alcohol on his hot breath. She turned her head, directing him to her neck. He licked the side of her face, then went to sucking on her neck while pulling at her shirt and fondling her breasts. He licked his tongue up the middle of her cleavage and nibbled on her.

BG pulled out all of his old tactics, but Mica's mind was running a mile a minute, trying to put together her next move. A feeling of guilt washed over her, and she silently wished I would understand that her only reason for allowing him to touch her was because her life was on the line. She remembered seeing her purse on the floor beside the futon and wondered if he had put her phone in it the way he used to always do when they were together. Mica knew if she could get in touch with me, I would come save her from the crazy. She also knew he would never let her get the phone willingly. So, Mica pretended to be really turned on by him. Thinking of me coming to save her made what she was doing easier. She started acting like he was driving her wild, breathing hard and moaning his name, begging him not to stop.

The crazed man got even more into it, believing his hostage's performance. He really thought he was driving her wild when, in truth, she was half squirming in disgust. Before he could remove her pants, she grabbed him by the hand, pulling it from between her legs. He glared at her, but she gave him a mischievous grin to make him relax again, then pulled his shirt off over his head. She began kissing down his chest while unbuckling his jeans. Anticipating what's to come, he kicked off his shoes and pants, then laid back, allowing her to take over from there.

Mica ran her tongue up his inner thighs, kissing her way in, fondling his balls as gently as she could, with her thoughts being to rip them off. BG's moans told her he approved. After all that licking and sucking, running her lips all the way up and down his shaft, it was time to make her move for the phone. She reached down and pulled the bag closer to her. While his moans and groans echoed through the room, she fished her free hand around inside her bag until her fingers found what she was searching for. Cupping the phone in her hand, Mica climbed on him, rubbing her warm center up and down his hardness and half-ass kissing him.

She remembered how much he liked getting lap dances, so she grinded herself onto him. All the while, behind his bliss-contorted face, she was desperately texting me her S.O.S. BG opened his eyes right away, spotting the phone in her hand through the mirror. He grabbed for the phone, cussing and shouting at her. When he jerked it out of her hand, he swung a right cross to her head. In that moment, Mica had no other thought but to save herself. Her body moved on fear's autopilot. With learned skill from their past fights, she blocked the blow by throwing her arm up against her face, protecting her head.

Even still, the force behind the blow had rocked her, but she managed to push herself off of him and onto her feet. Clearly enraged, he quickly stood up. Mica raised her fists in a fighting stance and stared him right in the eyes. She drew off the anger flowing through her, pushing down her fear and ready to release nothing but pure violence. Drawing strength from that, she prepared to fight her way to the door.

Moving slowly around the futon to create space between them, her eyes landed on a beer bottle. With lightning speed, she scooped it up and threw it at him. BG snapped his body sideways as the bottle flew past him and hit the wall. Not giving him time to react, Mica threw another one that hit him in the chest, then she charged at him.

With a loud, guttural scream, she mercilessly swung both arms in a windmill of fists that made him backpedal until he tripped and fell. Mica sidestepped to keep from tripping over him, and that's when she saw the phone on the floor. She quickly crossed the room and scooped it up on her way to the door.

"Mica, stop!" he yelled, snatching his pants and gun off the floor. "Bitch, stop before I blow yo' head off!" BG saw that she wasn't listening, so his weak ass shot at her.

Mica snatched the door open and ran out just as his shots whizzed by her, hitting the wall. She screamed and sped up. She didn't stop moving until she was outside of the house. She thought she heard him stumbling down the stairs coming for her, so she sprinted across the backyard. She cut through neighboring yards until she had to stop and catch her breath. Mica pressed herself against the side of a garage, praying that he didn't see which way she went. She dialed my number, willing me to answer.

Chapter 32

Leaving the crash site, a sudden nagging feeling came over me. I started to head over to Mica's place and wait for her to get in from work, so I could vent to her about what's going on. But I changed my mind and decided to go straight home. When I got to the crib, I fell across the bed, thinking, going through all of what's in my head. Hell yeah, I was stressing over the night's events. I had way too much to lose behind the bullshit Blackie and the goof troop were on with me. I was thinking of my next move and didn't even know I had fallen asleep. All I know is I was dragged awake by the ringing of my phone. Still a bit disoriented, I tapped "answer" without really opening my eyes.

"Hello?"

"Bae, you gotta come get me now! BG kidnapped me and—"

"Wait, wait . . . what? Mica, are you being serious right now?" I asked, sitting up in bed.

"Yes, I'm serious. He kidnapped me but I got away and he's still chasing me. I'm hiding in an alley somewhere on the South side, I think."

"I'm on my way, but I need you to tell me what street you're on so I can find you." I could hear the panic in her voice. "Do you think you can do that for me without him finding you?" I could kinda hear street traffic in her background. I was still dressed, so all I had to do was put on my shoes. "Are you okay? Did he hurt you?"

"Yeah . . . Hmmm, yeah, I'm okay. Bae, I'm not that far from the end of the alley. I'ma run over there and peek out."

"If you see a store or someplace that's open, go in there so you'll have people around 'til I get there." My heart pounded harder, listening to her moving.

"I'm so scared. Please don't get off the phone."

"I'm not. I need you to keep being strong and tell me where you are so I can get to you."

"I see a gas station. I'm on Greenfield, twenty-something and Greenfield. I can't see the street number from where I'm at."

"Okay, I think I know where you are. Get to the gas station and stay out of sight, but try to stay where somebody can see you just in case," I instructed as I rushed out the house with my keys and gun in hand. I had to take the Camaro because, in my haste, I grabbed the first set of keys my fingers touched. "How did he get you?" I inquired, now mad as hell that she was out there running for her life.

"He kept calling me nonstop, so I answered to tell him to stop calling my phone. Don't be mad, but I thought if I told him face-to-face he would get the point. Don't be mad."

"What the fuck, girl!" I got in the car and peeled off. "I get it, but you shouldn't have gone to say shit to him by yourself!" I exclaimed.

"I'm sorry, Bae. Please don't—"

"Stop talking! I need you to think." Anger turned my eyes as I sped through the early morning traffic rush, heading to the South side. I wasn't doing the dash, but I was surely pushing way past the speed limits. I shot past a police car and immediately their bright flashing lights were in my rearview mirrors. "Shit. Shit . . . Fuck!! Not now! Not fuckin' now!" I started to pull over but hearing Mica's panic in my ear made me turn down the first side street that I came to and once again dipped into an alley, shut off my lights, and waited for them to pass.

When I saw the cop car shoot by, I backed up out of the alley the way I came in to be sure I didn't repeat what happened to me earlier. It was all good. I made it to the gas station and spotted Mica flagging me down from beside one of the filling stations. I turned onto the lot and pulled to a stop beside her.

"Are you okay?" I asked as I was jumping out of the car, seeing her in tears, looking a mess.

"Look out!" she yelled, throwing her hands over her mouth in surprise at the sight of BG running up behind me.

"Yeah, wassup now, nigga!" I heard moments before I felt the muzzle of a gun pressed at the back of my head.

Not saying a word, I abruptly stepped back, slamming into him, then spun around, ducking under his gun hand and grabbed his arm. I locked up his elbow and used it to slam him to the ground. Then I leaped away from him and drew my own gun on him. All the while, the punk moved to re-aim his gun, but I was squeezing my trigger way before he could finish his thought.

I should have just broke that pussy-whipped punk's arm when I had the chance because it was my bad luck that the police were riding by the gas station right as the scuffle between us started. They jumped out on me with their guns aimed at my head. I instantly dropped my weapon, stepped away, and threw my hands up because it wasn't anything else I could do.

Mica, along with everyone else who witnessed what happened, tried to tell the police what happened, but they weren't hearing nothing. They forcibly slammed me to the ground and tightly handcuffed me. The next thing I knew, I was being hauled off to jail and booked in on a murder-one and gun possession charges. The rest is for another story. But I will say that it was like three years after I got to the joint that I broke things off with Mica. Why? Because it's hard enough having to do this time away from my babies and I don't need all of the extra that comes with tryna hold on to a guilt-locked relationship with the amount of time the judge gave me.

Now, y'all, I'ma fall back and chill. I'll holla at ya later . . .

Closure

Just because I tell you I love you doesn't mean I do. Saying that you want me to be honest with you is a lie. The truth is that you want my lies of wishful dreams. You want me to feed you false hope. To tell you that everything will be alright in the midst of war.

Just because I tell you I hate you doesn't mean I do. Saying that you can't live without me isn't true. You've survived years without me before me, and you will do the same after us. No, I don't hold you close. Saying that you need to feel my touch hurts. It tells me that we don't have a real connection. Having a split connection with one another is what's needed to stand the tests of doing time.

Just because you tell me you love me doesn't mean you do. Saying that to me is just your way of telling me that you feel you're obligated to do so. Because all of your procrastination towards our needs shows me that your words are not true.

Just because this is goodbye doesn't mean I won't say hi. Saying this is me giving your closure. We were friends in the beginning so we can be friends in this end…

Lock Down Publications and Ca$h Presents
Assisted Publishing Packages

Due to an increase in the price of services we have increased our prices. The prices below reflect the price increase as of 11/1/24.

BASIC PACKAGE $699 Editing Cover Design Formatting	UPGRADED PACKAGE $1000 Typing Editing Cover Design Formatting Upload eBooks to Amazon Upload Paperback to Amazon
ADVANCE PACKAGE $1,400 Typing Editing (line editing/content) Cover Design Formatting Copyright Registration Proofreading Upload eBooks to Amazon Upload Paperback to Amazon	LDP SUPREME PACKAGE $1,700 Typing Editing (line editing/content) Cover Design Formatting Copyright Registration Proofreading Set up Amazon Account Upload eBooks to Amazon Upload Paperback to Amazon Advertise on LDP's Amazon and Facebook Page

***

Other services available upon request.
Additional charges may apply

Lock Down Publications
P.O. Box 944
Stockbridge, GA 30281-9998
Phone: 470 303-9761
Email: lockdownpublications@gmail.com

Submission Guideline

Submit the first three chapters of your completed manuscript to ldpsubmissions@gmail.com. In the subject line add **Your Book's Title**. The manuscript must be in a Word Doc file and sent as an attachment. Document should be in Times New Roman, double spaced, and in size 12 font. Also, provide your synopsis and full contact information. If sending multiple submissions, they must each be in a separate email.

Have a story but no way to send it electronically? You can still submit to LDP/Ca$h Presents. Send in the first three chapters, written or typed, of your completed manuscript to:

LDP: Submissions Dept
P.O. Box 944
Stockbridge, GA 30281-9998

DO NOT send original manuscript. Must be a duplicate. Provide your synopsis and a cover letter containing your full contact information.

Thanks for considering LDP and Ca$h Presents.

NEW RELEASES

BLOODLINE OF A SAVAGE 1-3
THESE VICIOUS STREETS 1-3
RELENTLESS GOON 1-3
BY PRINCE A. TAUHID

THE BUTTERFLY MAFIA 1-3
BY FUMIYA PAYNE

A THUG'S STREET PRINCESS 1&2
BY MEESHA

CITY OF SMOKE 3
BY MOLOTTI

GET IT IN SLUGS 1 &2
BY B. STALL

STANDING ON HER BUSINESS 1&2
BY DG SANTANA

STEPPERS 1,2&3
THE REAL BADDIES OF CHI-RAQ
BY KING RIO

THE LANE 1&2
BY KEN-KEN SPENCE

THUG OF SPADES 1&2
LOVE IN THE TRENCHES 2
CORNER BOYS
BY COREY ROBINSON

TIL DEATH 3
BY ARYANNA

THE BIRTH OF A GANGSTER 4
BY DELMONT PLAYER

PRODUCT OF THE STREETS 1-3
BY DEMOND "MONEY" ANDERSON

NO TIME FOR ERROR
BY KEESE

MONEY HUNGRY DEMONS 1-2
BY TRANAY ADAMS

HUB CITY MENACE 1-3
BY J. WHITE

A THUGGISH PASSION 1&2
LAND OF DA HOOLIGANZ 1-4
KILLAZ ON STANDBY 1&2
BY IRA B.

FO'EVA ROLLIN 1&2
BY ASSA RAYMOND BAKER

THE LEVEL UP 1&3
BY LUXURY KING

Coming Soon from Lock Down Publications/Ca$h Presents

IF YOU CROSS ME ONCE 6
ANGEL V
By Anthony Fields

A THUGS STREET PRINCESS 3
By Meesha

CORNER BOYS 2
By Corey Robinson

THA TAKEOVER
By Keith Chandler

BETRAYAL OF A G 2
By Ray Vinci

SAVAGE FAMILY EMPIRE 1&2
SOULLESS GOON 1,2&3
THE DIRTY SIDE OF MONEY 1,2&3
By Prince

FOR MY ENEMY'S SAKE
AMBITIONS OF A SLIDER
FRESH OFF DA PORCH
By IRA B.

BY THE TRUCKLOAD 1-4
TIPPIN' THE SCALES 1-3
BAD BITCHES WIT GUNZ 3
PROBLEM SOLVED 2
By Christopher "Diesel" Hornezes

Available Now

RESTRAINING ORDER 1 & 2
By **CA$H & Coffee**

LOVE KNOWS NO BOUNDARIES 1-3
By **Coffee**

RAISED AS A GOON I, II, III & IV
BRED BY THE SLUMS I, II, III
BLAST FOR ME I & II
ROTTEN TO THE CORE I II III
A BRONX TALE I, II, III
DUFFLE BAG CARTEL I II III IV V VI
HEARTLESS GOON I II III IV V
A SAVAGE DOPEBOY I II
DRUG LORDS I II III
CUTTHROAT MAFIA I II
KING OF THE TRENCHES
By **Ghost**

LAY IT DOWN I & II
LAST OF A DYING BREED I II
BLOOD STAINS OF A SHOTTA I & II III
By **Jamaica**

LOYAL TO THE GAME I II III
LIFE OF SIN I, II III
By **TJ & Jelissa**

IF LOVING HIM IS WRONG…I & II
LOVE ME EVEN WHEN IT HURTS I II III
By **Jelissa**

PUSH IT TO THE LIMIT
By **Bre' Hayes**

BLOODY COMMAS I & II
SKI MASK CARTEL I, II & III
KING OF NEW YORK I II, III IV V
RISE TO POWER I II III
COKE KINGS I II III IV V
BORN HEARTLESS I II III IV
KING OF THE TRAP I II
By **T.J. Edwards**

WHEN THE STREETS CLAP BACK I & II III
THE HEART OF A SAVAGE I II III IV
MONEY MAFIA I II
LOYAL TO THE SOIL I II III
By **Jibril Williams**

A DISTINGUISHED THUG STOLE MY HEART I II & III
LOVE SHOULDN'T HURT I II III IV
RENEGADE BOYS 1-4
PAID IN KARMA 1-3
SAVAGE STORMS 1-3
AN UNFORESEEN LOVE 1-3
BABY, I'M WINTERTIME COLD 1-3
A THUG'S STREET PRINCESS 1&2
By **Meesha**

A GANGSTER'S CODE 1-3
A GANGSTER'S SYN 1-3
THE SAVAGE LIFE 1-3
CHAINED TO THE STREETS 1-3
BLOOD ON THE MONEY 1-3
A GANGSTA'S PAIN 1-3
BEAUTIFUL LIES AND UGLY TRUTHS
CHURCH IN THESE STREETS
By **J-Blunt**

CUM FOR ME 1-8
An LDP Erotica Collaboration

BLOOD OF A BOSS 1-5
SHADOWS OF THE GAME
TRAP BASTARD
By **Askari**

THE STREETS BLEED MURDER 1-3
THE HEART OF A GANGSTA 1-3
By **Jerry Jackson**

WHEN A GOOD GIRL GOES BAD
By **Adrienne**

THE COST OF LOYALTY 1-3
By **Kweli**

BRIDE OF A HUSTLA 1-3
THE FETTI GIRLS 1-3
CORRUPTED BY A GANGSTA 1-4
BLINDED BY HIS LOVE
THE PRICE YOU PAY FOR LOVE 1-3
DOPE GIRL MAGIC 1-3
By **Destiny Skai**

A KINGPIN'S AMBITION
A KINGPIN'S AMBITION II
I MURDER FOR THE DOUGH
By **Ambitious**

TRUE SAVAGE 1-7
DOPE BOY MAGIC 1-3
MIDNIGHT CARTEL 1-3
CITY OF KINGZ 1&2
NIGHTMARE ON SILENT AVE
THE PLUG OF LIL MEXICO 1&2
CLASSIC CITY
By **Chris Green**

A GANGSTER'S REVENGE 1-4
THE BOSS MAN'S DAUGHTERS 1-5
A SAVAGE LOVE 1&2
BAE BELONGS TO ME 1&2
A HUSTLER'S DECEIT 1-3
WHAT BAD BITCHES DO 1-3
SOUL OF A MONSTER 1-3
KILL ZONE
A DOPE BOY'S QUEEN 1-3
TIL DEATH 1-3
IMMA DIE BOUT MINE 1-6
DYING FOR LIKES
By **Aryanna**

A DOPEBOY'S PRAYER
By **Eddie "Wolf" Lee**

THE KING CARTEL 1-3
By **Frank Gresham**

THESE NIGGAS AIN'T LOYAL 1-3
By **Nikki Tee**

GANGSTA SHYT 1-3
By **CATO**

THE ULTIMATE BETRAYAL
By **Phoenix**

BOSS'N UP 1-3
By **Royal Nicole**

I LOVE YOU TO DEATH
By **Destiny J**

I RIDE FOR MY HITTA
I STILL RIDE FOR MY HITTA
By **Misty Holt**

LOVE & CHASIN' PAPER
By **Qay Crockett**

TO DIE IN VAIN
SINS OF A HUSTLA
By **ASAD**

BROOKLYN HUSTLAZ
By **Boogsy Morina**

BROOKLYN ON LOCK 1 & 2
By **Sonovia**

GANGSTA CITY
By **Teddy Duke**

A DRUG KING AND HIS DIAMOND 1-3
A DOPEMAN'S RICHES
HER MAN, MINE'S TOO 1&2
CASH MONEY HO'S
THE WIFEY I USED TO BE 1&2
PRETTY GIRLS DO NASTY THINGS
By **Nicole Goosby**

LIPSTICK KILLAH 1-3
CRIME OF PASSION 1-3
FRIEND OR FOE 1-3
By **Mimi**

TRAPHOUSE KING 1-3
KINGPIN KILLAZ 1-3
STREET KINGS 1&2
PAID IN BLOOD 1&2
CARTEL KILLAZ 1-3
DOPE GODS 1&2
By **Hood Rich**

THE STREETS ARE CALLING
By **Duquie Wilson**

STEADY MOBBN' 1-3
THE STREETS STAINED MY SOUL 1-3
By **Marcellus Allen**

WHO SHOT YA 1-3
SON OF A DOPE FIEND 1-4
HEAVEN GOT A GHETTO 1&2
SKI MASK MONEY 1&2
By **Renta**

GORILLAZ IN THE BAY 1-4
TEARS OF A GANGSTA 1/&2
3X KRAZY 1&2
STRAIGHT BEAST MODE 1&2
By **DE'KARI**

TRIGGADALE 1-3
MURDA WAS THE CASE 1-3
By **Elijah R. Freeman**

SLAUGHTER GANG 1-3
RUTHLESS HEART 1-3
By **Willie Slaughter**

GOD BLESS THE TRAPPERS 1-3
THESE SCANDALOUS STREETS 1-3
FEAR MY GANGSTA 1-5
THESE STREETS DON'T LOVE NOBODY 1-2
BURY ME A G 1-5
A GANGSTA'S EMPIRE 1-4
THE DOPEMAN'S BODYGAURD 1&2
THE REALEST KILLAZ 1-3
THE LAST OF THE OGS 1-3
By **Tranay Adams**

MARRIED TO A BOSS 1-3
By **Destiny Skai & Chris Green**

KINGZ OF THE GAME 1-7
CRIME BOSS 1-4
By **Playa Ray**

FUK SHYT
By **Blakk Diamond**

DON'T F#CK WITH MY HEART 1&2
By **Linnea**

ADDICTED TO THE DRAMA 1-3
IN THE ARM OF HIS BOSS
By **Jamila**

LOYALTY AIN'T PROMISED 1&2
By **Keith Williams**

YAYO 1-4
A SHOOTER'S AMBITION 1&2
BRED IN THE GAME
By **S. Allen**

TRAP GOD 1-3
RICH $AVAGE 1-3
MONEY IN THE GRAVE 1-3
CARTEL MONEY 1&2
By **Martell Troublesome Bolden**

FOREVER GANGSTA 1&2
GLOCKS ON SATIN SHEETS 1&2
By **Adrian Dulan**

TOE TAGZ 1-4
LEVELS TO THIS SHYT 1&2
IT'S JUST ME AND YOU
By **Ah'Million**

KINGPIN DREAMS 1-3
RAN OFF ON DA PLUG
By **Paper Boi Rari**

THE STREETS MADE ME 1-3
By **Larry D. Wright**

CONFESSIONS OF A GANGSTA 1-4
CONFESSIONS OF A JACKBOY 1-3
CONFESSIONS OF A HITMAN
CONFESSIONS OF A DOPE BOY
By **Nicholas Lock**

I'M NOTHING WITHOUT HIS LOVE
SINS OF A THUG
TO THE THUG I LOVED BEFORE
A GANGSTA SAVED XMAS
IN A HUSTLER I TRUST
By **Monet Dragun**

QUIET MONEY 1-3
THUG LIFE 1-3
EXTENDED CLIP 1&2
A GANGSTA'S PARADISE
By **Trai'Quan**

CAUGHT UP IN THE LIFE 1-3
THE STREETS NEVER LET GO 1-3
By **Robert Baptiste**

NEW TO THE GAME 1-3
MONEY, MURDER & MEMORIES 1-3
By **Malik D. Rice**

CREAM 2-3
THE STREETS WILL TALK
By **Yolanda Moore**

THE STREETS WILL NEVER CLOSE 1-3
By **K'ajji**

LIFE OF A SAVAGE 1-4
A GANGSTA'S QUR'AN 1-4
MURDA SEASON 1-3
GANGLAND CARTEL 1-3
CHI'RAQ GANGSTAS 1-4
KILLERS ON ELM STREET 1-3
JACK BOYZ N DA BRONX 1-3
A DOPEBOY'S DREAM 1-3
JACK BOYS VS DOPE BOYS 1-3
COKE GIRLZ
COKE BOYS
SOSA GANG 1&2
BRONX SAVAGES
BODYMORE KINGPINS
BLOOD OF A GOON
By **Romell Tukes**

CONCRETE KILLA 1-3
VICIOUS LOYALTY 1-3
BLOODY MONEY BAGS
By **Kingpen**

THE ULTIMATE SACRIFICE 1-6
KHADIFI
IF YOU CROSS ME ONCE 1-3
ANGEL 1-4
IN THE BLINK OF AN EYE
By **Anthony Fields**

THE LIFE OF A HOOD STAR
By **Ca$h & Rashia Wilson**

NIGHTMARES OF A HUSTLA 1-3
BLOOD AND GAMES 1&2
By **King Dream**

GHOST MOB
By **Stilloan Robinson**

HARD AND RUTHLESS 1&2
MOB TOWN 251
THE BILLIONAIRE BENTLEYS 1-3
REAL G'S MOVE IN SILENCE
By **Von Diesel**

MOB TIES 1-7
SOUL OF A HUSTLER, HEART OF A KILLER 1-3
GORILLAZ IN THE TRENCHES
OOPS CRY TOO 1&2
THE DAUGHTER OF A CARTEL BOSS
By **SayNoMore**

BODYMORE MURDERLAND 1-3
THE BIRTH OF A GANGSTER 1-4
By **Delmont Player**

FOR THE LOVE OF A BOSS 1&2
By **C. D. Blue**

KILLA KOUNTY 1-5
TENDER
By **Khufu**

MOBBED UP 1-4
THE BRICK MAN 1-5
THE COCAINE PRINCESS 1-10
STEPPERS 1-3
SUPER GREMLIN 1-4
A GANGSTA'S SON
By **King Rio**

MONEY GAME 1&2
By **Smoove Dolla**

A GANGSTA'S KARMA 1-5
By **FLAME**

KING OF THE TRENCHES 1-3
By **GHOST & TRANAY ADAMS**

BAD BITCHES WIT GUNZ 1&2
PROBLEM SOLVED
By "Christopher Diesel" Hornezes

QUEEN OF THE ZOO 1&2
By **Black Migo**

GRIMEY WAYS 1-3
BETRAYAL OF A G
By **Ray Vinci**

XMAS WITH AN ATL SHOOTER
By **Ca$h & Destiny Skai**

KING KILLA 1&2
By **Vincent "Vitto" Holloway**

BETRAYAL OF A THUG 1&2
By **Fre$h**

COUNTDOWN OF A KILLA 1&2
SEX, MURDER AND GOD 1&2
GUNS DOWN, BOTTOMS UP 1&2
By Lo-Life

THE MURDER QUEENS 1-7
By **Michael Gallon**

FOR THE LOVE OF BLOOD 1-4
By **Jamel Mitchell**

FO'EVA ROLLIN' 4 | ASSA RAYMOND BAKER

HOOD CONSIGLIERE 1&2
NO TIME FOR ERROR
By **Keese**

PROTÉGÉ OF A LEGEND 1,2&3
LOVE IN THE TRENCHES 1&2
By **Corey Robinson**

THE PLUG'S RUTHLESS DAUGHTER 1&2
By **Tony Daniels**

BORN IN THE GRAVE 1-3
CRIME PAYS
By **Self Made Tay**

MOAN IN MY MOUTH
By **XTASY**

TORN BETWEEN A GANGSTER AND A GENTLEMAN
By **J-BLUNT & Miss Kim**

LOYALTY IS EVERYTHING 1-3
CITY OF SMOKE 1-3
By **Molotti**

HERE TODAY GONE TOMORROW 1&2
By **Fly Rock**

WOMEN LIE MEN LIE 1-4
FIFTY SHADES OF SNOW 1-3
STACK BEFORE YOU SPLURGE
GIRLS FALL LIKE DOMINOES
NAÏVE TO THE STREETS
By **ROY MILLIGAN**

PILLOW PRINCESS
By **S. Hawkins**

THE BUTTERFLY MAFIA 1-3
SALUTE MY SAVAGERY 1&2
By **Fumiya Payne**

THE LANE 1&2
By Ken-Ken Spence

THE PUSSY TRAP 1-5
By **Nene Capri**

DIRTY DNA
By **Blaque**

SANCTIFIED AND HORNY
by **XTASY**

BOOKS BY LDP'S CEO, CA$H

TRUST IN NO MAN
TRUST IN NO MAN 2
TRUST IN NO MAN 3
BONDED BY BLOOD
SHORTY GOT A THUG
THUGS CRY
THUGS CRY 2
THUGS CRY 3
TRUST NO BITCH
TRUST NO BITCH 2
TRUST NO BITCH 3
TIL MY CASKET DROPS
RESTRAINING ORDER
RESTRAINING ORDER 2
IN LOVE WITH A CONVICT
LIFE OF A HOOD STAR
XMAS WITH AN ATL SHOOTER